VAMPIRE HERO SAGA

WELCOME BACK

TO

MY

UNIVERSE

SHANE

OTHER BOOKS BY THIS AUTHOR:

DESTINY'S KEY: 2008

BREATH OF MAGIK: 2009

THE VAMPIRE WARS: Beginning 2009

ENTER THE GUARDIANS: KYL 2009

GUARDIANS- LOST ON GROT: 2009

BLOOD BY DAY 2009 (VAMPIRE HERO)

SHADOWS REVENGE 2009 (VMP HERO)

BLACK WINGS: 2009

WORLD OF ICE 2009

HOUSE OF THE WOLF: TBA

VAMPIRE WARS: 2 TBA

SHANE

Distributed through LULU.com

First printing March 2009
Book Printed in America

ISBN: 978-0-578-03095-1

**COVER ART BY W. SHANE WILSON
ALL RIGHTS RESERVED.**

SHANE

VAMPIRE HERO SAGA

SHADOWS REVENGE

BOOK TWO

VAMPIRE HERO SAGA

W. SHANE WILSON

SHANE

SHANE

Welcome back Vampire lovers, we are continuing our journey with the boys and their crew to try to change the world and let the magic back into the world.

SPECIAL THANKS TO AJAY, PEGI, AND JACY FOR CONTINUING TO PLAY A ROLE IN OUR SAGA. THANKS FOR THE SUPPORT AND INSPIRATION.

TO MY ARLENE, JOSTON AND JESSICA
I HOPE YOU WILL ALWAYS LOVE MY STORIES.

SHANE

SHANE

TABLE OF CHAPTERS;

SHANE

SHANE

OPENING

In a castle in a small Irish township, the lord of all of Europe sits drinking wine with his vineyard master in the great hall of O'Day Keep. This is a regular tradition with every harvest and wine making. Collin O'Day, who is a twelve hundred year old vampire, loves human food and wine. He is a good lord as well; he is not in the habit of letting his subject be eaten by rogue vampires or anything else. His Wine master knows what Collin is and loves the man anyway. His family has served the House of the O'Day clan for as long as they have existed and never has even one of his family been harmed. Amus Savage was a portly man with a happy face, he was in his forty fifth year of life. He was wealthy by most men's standard but his friendship with Collin was his prized possession. Collin felt the same way about Amus.

(GONG)

The door gong that Collin brought back from China when he visited his friend the Khan, whom ruled Asia like he did Europe, just bonged, so the servants went to announce whom ever came to call. There was a crashing noise and one of the servants came bouncing into Collin's view bleeding. Collin was very kind to his staff, and anyone who injured them just signed a death sentence. In a flash Collin burst to speed.

"Geet out of me wee, or I'll kill ya" A vampire screamed!

SHANE

Collin had the black-heart by the throat; then he let him go in disgust.

"I thought I banished you from my lands" Collin announced loudly.

"True but a new hunter came and burned Brian and me out in America; He seems to be determined to wipe out all vampires, from the top down. I came to warn you" Mark said.

Collin looked over Mark and was unpleased as usual. He could not understand how his blood could flow through this trash before him.

"I will grant you a short stay in my lands, until I can confirm or abolish the news you brought me. One more thing" Collin said as he back handed Mark into a stone wall. "You will not touch my staff or any other human in Europe or I will cut your heart out personally. Do you understand me"?

"Yes sir, I will obey you" Mark said quickly.

Secretly Mark had hoped that Brian would challenge his Great grandfather to a duel and kill him, thus mark would become Lord O'day over Europe. However, Brian did not want to risk it, Collin was not to be trifled with; he killed every opponent he had ever had and was old and extremely powerful. Collin was soft toward Humans; that would someday spell his doom, maybe that day had come. Mark had set in motion the wheels that would bring then Hunter Jazon here to Ireland. Collin would not allow a hunter on his lands, so they would be sure to kill each other, or at the least one would parish. Life was good mark thought.

SHANE

SHANE

CHAPTER ONE: HEATHROW

Ajay had nothing to say the entire flight. The young proud black man was carrying around a burden of guilt; that was not his to carry. Ajay would likely transfer the debt properly when he met up with Mark O'Day.

"Hey, wonder if there are any hot wolf girls on this side of the pond; as they say?" Jc asked.

"Your on guard duty; so no booty." Terry said.

All four men laughed; it was good to laugh again; even for something stupid. Ajay was the first to go back to silence. Jazon could tell that his closest friend was so deeply disturbed that nothing short of genocide was going to bring him around. If Silky died; then Ajay would hunt every blood sucker on the planet...and eventually Jazon as well. Jazon would cross that bridge when it came up.

"Hey man, how are we going to find Brian and his leech in the whole of Europe anyway?" Terry asked.

Everyone looked art Jazon and he shocked them by smiling; which displayed his deadly fangs.

"Oh, I think they will find us or leave us some clues. They don't want to get away; if they did; they would not have left a message telling us where they went." Jazon explained.

SHANE

"Trap?" Ajay said.

"Yeppers, they are going to draw us in and close the trap on us. However, since we know it is a trap; it is unlikely that we will be caught by it." Jazon explained.

"Let's hope that is right." Jc said.

(SNARL)

Terry was across the plane an in Jc's face; with his claws extended. Jc was caught off guard and was pinned with Terry's claws at his throat. Jc's eyes turned red and he was getting hairy; when a hand pulled Terry back softly, but firmly.

"Calm down Terry." Jazon said.

"He is questioning your leadership! I will not tolerate a traitor in our ranks!" Terry bellowed.

"He has not been through the ringer with us Terry. Jc does not have the same point of view you do about me and Ajay, because we have bled together and we have had to rely on each other to survive. Give Jc a shot at being part of the team; he has been stuck in Brian's grasp for a long time and needs to learn to breathe and trust his partners. Beside he is a smart ass and did not mean anything by his comments at all. You just over reacted." Jazon said.

Jc was surprised at the ease at which Jazon put Terry on his heels; without testing his pride or honor.

Jazon just subtly talked the angry wolf down, and the wolf did not seem to mind at all.

Jc was not use to having a vampire as a boss who actually cared about his crew and how they worked together. This Jazon Wild was a strange man.

(IN LONDON)

The private plane landed in the wee hours of the night and the London Bobbies came out to meet it. When the door opened, Ajay was about to walk out the door when Jc yanked him back and held him.

"What...?" Ajay started to yell.

A poison dart was lodged in the wall right where Ajay had just been standing. Jc only shrugged his shoulders and smiled. Ajay gave him a punch in the arm and a nod.

"So, we are expected; I see." Jazon said.

"So it would seem little brother. Shall we go meet them?" Ajay asked.

Before either of them could discuss the issue, Terry went out the lower escape hatch and bowled over the ten Bobbies. The cop tried to get up but; Terry roared and his eyes changed; so they Bobbies stayed put.

"He is a handy one; isn't he?" Jc said.

SHANE

The trio left the plane and walked down to where the Bobbies were pinned to the ground in fear. Jazon looked them all over and then he spoke to the wolves.

"Sniff them' one of these jokers tried to kill my brother, that can't go unpunished." Jazon said.

Jc and Terry sniffed the Bobbies and so did Jazon. They seemed unsatisfied after the job was complete. Ajay smiled and stepped forward.

"Hey Bobbies, we are not your enemies; however' one of you tried to kill me; so we have to find them for safety sake. Which one of you is not know to the others? Go on, sit up and look at each other, is there anyone that you don't know/" Ajay asked.

The sergeant sat up and looked at the men and some of the others did the same. All of them spotted the one who was not one of them instantly. That guy bolted at inhuman speed toward the dark throughway on the left. Terry made to follow but Jc grabbed his forearm.

"Think before you act Terry; poison darts of unknown origins. Besides kid; it is a obvious trap. Jc said.

The words were more true than Jc knew. The throughway was filled with traps and explosives. The wolf could have made it beyond the blast area, but they assassin would have caught him at the end in a death trap. Jc saved Terry for a bit of bother as the Brits say.

SHANE

The sergeant got to his feet looking rather embarrassed by the whole mess. The other Bobbies got up as well.

"Well, um, sorry about that Governor. Seems we have had a bit of a mishap. (Chuckle). Welcome to England...such as it is." The sergeant said.

All four of the Yanks looked at each other and then they busted out laughing, it startled the Bobbies somewhat. Jazon regained his senses and reassured the cops.

"Sorry, it is just a long running bad joke; you see there is always someone trying to kill us; so we are use to this kind of thing. Anyway, why is there a squat of police here to meet our plane?" Jazon said.

"Sir Alister sent word that his plane was coming in and there would be important personnel on it. Where are the dignitaries sir?" The Bobbie asked.

"Sir Alister?" Terry asked.

"Alister told them we were important; because we are important. We have a duty to hunt down Brian Finney and Mark O'Day and put them both in the dirt face down." Ajay said in anger.

"Were you supposed to take us somewhere, or toss us some information Sarge?" Jc asked.

The Bobbie looked ill for a moment and shook as if he were about to die. Jazon noticed most of the police

SHANE

were green as well. None of them seemed to be able to speak.

"Did...did you say O'Day, as in Collin O'Day?" The sergeant asked.

"We don't know anything about a Collin, we are after a punk named Mark, same last name perhaps; but not likely to be related unless this Collin fellow is a dirt bag." Ajay said.

"Nay, Collin O'Day is a grand man and he is the Lord of most of Europe and he literally rules Ireland lads. If it is in yer minds lads to stir up some mischief where Lord O'Day is involved; don't do it; he is not to be trifled with." The sergeant said.

"Look mate, we are tired and angry at present; and we would like to rest and eat; if you follow my meaning." Jc said in a gruff tone.

The Bobbies looked at each other and then they pulled out pistols and pointed them at Jazon and the boys.

"You better come with us for your own good; that is until we can get your plane fueled up and send you home again. You are all way to young to die." The sergeant said.

It was the last thing he heard before he hit the ground. Jazon drove into the middle of the Bobbie and brought his hand in tight to his chest as he moved; as he came to a stop so fast nobody saw him move; he threw his arms opened wide. All the Bobbies were knocked flat in a near perfect circle. Jazon looked around and all the men began to tremble in mortal fear. Jazon's eyes were a brilliant color of glowing lite crimson. Since it was dark when they landed; Jazon's eyes were like search lights over the coast. Worse, the two werewolves transformed and were snarling only millimeters away from the London police squad.

"Boys back off a little; you are scaring the Bobbies to death. Now listen up gentlemen; because I am not going to repeat this. I am not your enemy; keep it that way. We do not require your protection; we are more than capable of looking after our own hides; as you can plainly see." Jazon said calmly.

Ajay walked over and grabbed the sergeant off the ground and held him dangling by his coat. Ajay shook him hard a few times and then spoke.

"I am looking for a murdering piece of crap, if you know where he is and don't tell me; then I will find you and kill you!" Ajay growled in the man's terrified face.

"I dun not know hem." The sergeant said in sudden deep accent.

"You're an Irishman." Jc said.

"Aye, I am." The scared man said.

Jazon looked at Jc and smiled; although the wolf did not know why. However, Ajay did know why and he smiled also.

SHANE

"Take me to your lord Collin O'Day." Jazon said.

(FROM THE SHADOWS)

The small twelve year old frame of a boy was watching the scene play out. He saw one vampire and two wolves. The black man he was not sure about, he was very strong and fast but that could be from training hard. The boy hated vampires so passionately; that even at his tender age he hunted them without any mercy and lived to tell the tale. One of the wolves turned and looked into the shadows, he clearly saw the boy; who flipped him off. The wolf laughed to himself; which confused the boy. Weren't wolves supposed to be mad dogs? A small rustling behind the boy made him spin silver knife at the ready under his over sized sleeves. It was a drunkard falling over at the mouth of the alley, the boy was not happy about this. It was likely a trap. He now had death in both directions. When the boy turned to look back at the vampire and his wolves; he found himself looking at the chest of the younger smaller wolf. The werewolf made no move tot touch or attack him. He did not even look down; his dreamy eyes were glued to the drunk in the alley.

"That is not a man over there kid; and he is not drunk; there is no smell of booze on him. It is a trap however...for you or us. I wonder?" Terry said.

The boy felt oddly safe next to this monster and that scared him. He had his knife in line with the wolf's

SHANE

throat and could plunge it home at anytime. The boy looked away and followed the wolf's gaze; it went to the person laying in the alley. The boy suddenly saw what the wolf did. The eyes of the drunk were slightly glowing.

"Shit...they are after me!" The boy said.

"What; why would a monster be after you kid?" Terry asked.

"I kill vampires mate, and they don't like that much. I lived this long by keeping out of sight and picking one off at a time. I think that one over there is not the only one." The boy said.

"Fine, then you are with us kid." Terry said as he grabbed the boy and made like a flash of lightning.

   The boy was put on his feet in the middle of the Bobbies who looked at the boy and one reached for him, only to have his arm knocked away by Terry.

"He is with me." Terry said as his eyes turned a nice shade of no touchy yellow orange.

   The boy was a known thief and the police wanted him pretty bad; because he stole high priced items made of the purest silver. The Bobbies wanted to argue but the sergeant told them to shut up and fall in to ranks because they were leaving.

"Good luck to you my young friend, you'll be needing it." The sergeant said.

SHANE

Jazon stepped in front of the man and was promptly shot in the stomach with a silver bullet. Jazon smiled and leaned in closure.

"I believe you were going to introduce me to Collin? If you shoot me again I am going to toss you a beaten." Jazon told him.

In the end the Bobbie left the sergeant on his orders and marched away. The pilot of Alister's plane; who watched the entire scene told Jazon he would have the plane ready to go whenever he said. Jazon shook the man's hand and told him to watch his back and thank you.

Terry was enjoying the kid. Terry was the youngest wolf in the pack and it was nice to feel like the big brother for once. The boy was quiet and he looked over Jazon with intense hatred. Terry noticed the look and chuckled.

"Lil' buddy; with all the weapons you can carry or imagine; you could not beat that guy." Terry said.

"My name is Payton not little bubby. You would be surprised what I can do; if I must. You are a wolf are you not? I thought werewolves were the slaves of vampires, yet you seem like friends to me; I do not understand this?" the boy explained.

"Yes, I am a werewolf. No, I am not his slave, and yes I am his friend. Jazon is like no man I have ever known. He is selfless and kind and the most fierce unstoppable vampire killer whoever lived." Terry said.

Payton started to speak and then he looked at Jazon and then at Ajay with an extreme case of confused, the big wolf kid said that the vampire was a vampire killer? That did not make any sense at all. Why would the vampire kill his own kind? Maybe he wanted their territories; yes that was it.

"Payton, do you know anything about a man named Mark O'Day, I wish to find him and kill him?" Jazon said.

"Not if I get to him first bro." Ajay said.

Payton was shocked by the face of the vampire in front of him. He had kind eyes that were a strange mix of brown and red, and he smelled like Rootbeer, and not blood. What was up with this guy?

"I don't get you guys. Are you a human or are you like them monsters?" Payton asked.

"I am a full human; Jazon is my best friend and brother. He is very special Payton, and so are these two. We all hunt together for the bad vampires and monsters that prey on innocent blood; whether it is human or magical creatures." Ajay explained.

"What; do you mean to tell me that there are more than just blood suckers and wolves out there?" Payton said grey faced.

(All four of the boys laughed at once).

SHANE

"We're sorry bud, it is just that we have fought so hard and bled so much lately that the question was just ironic and funny to us." Terry said.

"I was recently the enforcer for the Prince of Portland; and I hated his guts. He held me in slavery by holding my best friend hostage. She died before I could find her and rescue her. I will live always with that shame. I will no longer let any vampire or anyone else use me." Jc said as his eyes grew very hard and black.

Payton was more confused now than ever. Why didn't the vampire eat the human, and why would to free wolves follow this blood sucker. Nothing made any sense. Payton jumped up and stabbed Jazon in the heart with his silver knife.

"Well isn't this magical." Jazon said.

Payton was beyond shocked; he felt mortal fear to the core of his existence. Why didn't the blood sucker die when I stabbed him?
"HEY!" Terry roared and reached for the boy.

Jazon grabbed his arm and held it still and looked at Terry and shook his head no. Then he looked at Payton.

"He is never going to trust us if he is always afraid of us. Look Payday; I am not a regular vampire; silver, garlic, holy water and so on do nothing to me kiddo; I am immune. Here check this out." Jazon said as he pulled his silver cross out of his shirt and showed it to Payton.

SHANE

"What...that does not make sense!" Payton said with angry tears in his eyes.

"It is my fate to look after the weak and helpless kid, I gave my word; my oath to GOD that is would protect the innocent from other vampires and their allies. Now pull your knife out of my chest please." Jazon said.

Payton pulled the knife out of Jazon's chest and smelled it. The boys watched him; and then the kid tasted Jazon's blood and was startled. Payton turned his eyes on Jazon and they were wild with emotion.

"Everything that I knew is shit; I don't know what to believe anymore; you just shattered my beliefs and my drive; now what the hell am I going to do." Payton screamed at Jazon.

"What brought that on man?" Ajay asked.

"His blood is alive, he is not undead. He does not have the vampire poison in his blood. He... he can't be a vampire!" Payton said through clenched teeth.

"Well tough shit about you ideals kid; we are at war. Where Jazon and Ajay are concerned, normal does not apply as far as I have seen. Ajay is a pure human, but he steps aside for no man nor beast; he has fought to the point of his own death. Jazon is much the same; he takes the lead on all of our raids and places himself in the front of the danger before he will risk any one of his friends. All the wolf packs in the states know his name and he has been mark as a beware of person; if you want to start some trouble." Jc said.

SHANE

The group sat on the private bus and pondered their personal thoughts quietly as the sergeant lead the boys to see a man who could introduce them to Collin O'Day. The sergeant did not want any part of this. Collin was held to be a good man; however, his retribution if he felt crossed; was shift and brutal. The thief boy sat next to the smart mouthed big kid and they seemed to have bonded. The big hair guy was watching the vampire intensely as if he were trying to decide something important; or to discover something important. Jazon was on the phone with someone. Ajay had his headphones on and his eyes closed; but he seemed alert despite that fact.

The bus stopped out side of a hotel and the sergeant got out; the boys followed. They enter the hotel and it was plush as plush could be. The sergeant was shaking in fear when they walked in. A huge man was walking toward them at a slow rolling gate. He had on a black suit that made it impossible to tell if he was fat or a rack of muscles; and he walk was no help. The kid settled the matter for the group.

"Hello lard ass; I told you I would get you in the end." Payton said with a smile.

The large man actually looked shocked and fear went across his massive face. He locked his jaw and charged like a bull elephant. He was not fat, not even close to fat. The kid went into an elaborate dance and drew blades out of thin air, as he went down the hallway toward the charging mammoth. The boy looked like his might get himself killed so Terry launch himself

SHANE

into the elephant and the shock wave from the impact made the walls crack. The elephants eyes changed to blue and he tried to push passed Terry to get at Payton; but Terry had him in grid lock and he could not reach the boy. All the time Payton taunted the elephant with insults and threats.

"Sheez, will somebody do something with that damned kid!" Terry snarled.

"I WILL KILL YOU!" the elephant screamed in a tiny little voice, like a small girl.

All time stopped for a moment as they boys looked at each other and then burst into uncontrollable laughter. The elephant stepped back and looked at the group in general dismay. He did not however attack.

"Look big guy; we did not come here to listen to you sing, we did come here so we could meet Collin O'Day." Jc said in a smart ass tone, and then snickered.

The boys watched the man with expert eyes, even Payton who had deadly blades in both hands looked ready to rock at a moments notice.

"Fine; come this way; it is your funeral." The elephant said.

They followed the big man down the hallway to a door with gold lettering; that was real gold. The big man opened the door and entered. Terry pushed the door open wide all the way to make sure no person was behind the door; looking to bushwhack them. Ajay walked in next and Jc could tell his hand was gripping his shotgun. Payton and Jc walked in together with Jazon hot on his hills. Ajay looked at Jazon who had rust red eyes; that meant there were supernatural creatures here. Suddenly Jazon's eyes went deep crimson.

"Oh Snap!" Ajay said as he yanked the shotgun out of his coat and turned it on the middle of the room where Jazon was looking.

In the middle of the room against a solid wood wall sat three men. The elephant addressed the man in the middle. He was a handsome man of maybe thirty and his long blond hair and blue eyes marked him as a vampire. The Asian man beside him was powerfully built and angry looking. However, the third man was Brian Finney, who looked shocked and afraid. Instantly the wolves changed into full werewolf mode. Jazon grabbed their fur and held them steady.

"No...not yet; first we talk business, and then you can kill Finney if it pleases you." Jazon said.

"You assume a great deal stranger; what makes you think you could kill Brian? What makes you think we would let you?" The Asian man said in a vicious way.

The room was startled by Jazon and Ajay's laughter. Ajay had tears in his eyes but was able to talk through the fits of insane laughter.

"What makes you think you could stop us Gus?" Ajay asked.

SHANE

The blond man spoke softly and without menace to try to regain the peace; that was not to be however.

"I think we can work this out; without blood shed. This man is the Prince of Portland and as such he can pay off any debt he may owe you." the blond said.

"Wrong; he is no longer the prince. I am the new king and this piece of trash attacked our mates like the coward he is. We have come to settle up. I might let him live if...if he gives me the cure to the poison he injected Silky with. It is his choice to make." Jazon said as his eyes turned white and his ear became pointed.

"I have heard enough." The Asian announced as he jumped up and made to attack.

(KABOOM)

Ajay jack a round into the chest of the Asian vampire; who foolishly thought he could take it. He went down and screamed in pain until he was nearly dead. Ajay went forward and was going to take his head off when Jazon stopped him.

"No, he is an arrogant ass, but he is not our enemy. Let him go Ajay.

"FINE, but I want Finney's head on a stick!" Ajay roared.

Payton had never seen a vampire put on his back so easily; what the hell was in that gun anyway. Payton saw the elephant reaching for a double headed axe, he did not know if he should say something or just nail the elephant with one of his knives. Payton was shook out of his concentration by Jazon's whispered voice in his ear.

"If he lifts that axe off the floor take him down Payday." Jazon said.

Payton looked at Jazon and the man was not even close to him; or looking at him or the elephant. Payton refocused on his target, just as the elephant lifted his weapon, the twelve year old moved like a seasoned killer. Before the elephant even knew what happened; the kid had impaled him at the base of the skull and the small of his back with silver knives. The elephant dropped the axe and screamed in pain. Just as he turned to see who his attacker was, Payton did a flying barrel roll flip and cut off the elephants head and impaled his heart. Payton stood back and looked at the man on the couch in a way that was unmistakable...you are next.

"I will grant you; your life; however, Brian is mine, please do not interfere with us or we will be forced to kill ya." Jazon said pleasantly.

Brian sat so still he seemed dead; which of course he was. The blond man stood up and spoke.

"We have a problem; you see this man is a guest in my house and as such I must actively protect him as the host. I might agree with your claim; however, I cannot allow you to take Brian from me...no matter the cost." The blond man said.

SHANE

The Asian man on the floor was trying to get up, but Ajay stepped on the back of his head and lowered his shotgun barrel down until it touched his bald head in a meaningful way.

"How about this dude, are you responsible for him as well?" Ajay asked.

"That is Ming; he is the nephew of Kahn; who rules all of Asia; you would do well not to make an enemy out of Kahn. I am sure that Ming would be willing to let all of this go like water under a bridge if you let him leave unharmed." The blond man said.

The boys all laughed; which scared the blond vampire and Brian. Ming was just plain pissed; because Ajay's size twelve's were on top of his bald head and so was the barrel of a shotgun.

"Do we look like idiots man? Well, we are not fools; and we are not asking you shit; we are taking Brian. The question posed to you is whether you and Ming here are going to live through this; not if we can take Brian; because he is already ours pal." Ajay said in a harsh tone.

The scene was as tense as could be. The boys; plus the kid were staring down the vampire in his own layer. The sergeant slipped out and disappeared into the night; he wanted no part of any of this mess. Ming stopped struggling and made a command decision.

SHANE

"Remove you footwear from my head black man and I will leave this building and not return; nor will I take any action against you. You have the word of the Kahn's nephew, and my word of honor." Ming said.

Ajay was not about to let Ming up but Jazon cleared his throat and motioned for Ajay to let the Chinese man up. Ajay stepped back and away. Ming got up very slow and looked into Ajay's eyes. Ming's eyes were a brilliant blue and he was deeply angry; however, he extended his hand to Ajay. Ajay had the shotgun aimed at Ming's chest; but he reached out and shook the vamps hand anyway.

"You are a brave man human; I will we never have to meet as foes; it would please me not to have to kill a good man such as yourself." Ming turned and looked at the blond man and then looked at Jazon. "You should asked Brian to leave your home; thus dissolving your need to protect him. This man is no mere vampire, he is more; I can feel it and so can you. We both know how strong Brian is and he is scared of this man; let that be your teacher alone." Ming said as he smiled at Jazon.

"Go in peace Ming and good journey to you." Jazon said.

The prince of Asia left per his word and did not return; although Jazon knew they would meet again. Jc snarled and turned to the door and instantly transformed fully into a werewolf. Jc was special even for a werewolf; he could be human, or a werewolf or a complete Timberwolf. He was a giant hulking werewolf now and he was set on the balls of his feet to launch himself in an instant. The blond man took this short distraction to attack. Darts came out of his sleeves and they were flung at blinding speed at each of the boys. In a blur of movement Jazon flung his leather jacket out and spun; the move deflected the darts harmlessly into the walls. Brian saw his chance to live and took it, his rammed his way right thru the wall and ran off into the night. Ajay would have went after him but the room was suddenly flooded with vampires; and they wanted to fight. Jazon grabbed Payton and tossed him to Terry. The werewolf shoved the boy behind him and went to work killing the two blood drinkers that charged him. Terry had worked on his close quarters combat with Wolf and Jazon, so he was patient and let them come in close enough they even if they tried to retreat he who nail them hard with one or both hands or a well placed foot.

The blond man sat down and was surprised to see Jazon sitting next to him.

"I should kill you; but I want you to call off your boys before they are all dead. None of you are equal to us; we will kill you all if we continue." Jazon said in a matter of fact voice.

Blond saw the truth of Jazon's words; his crew were being destroyed; not beaten, destroyed. He suddenly understood why Brian Finney feared this man.

"STOP, please, just stop fighting. It is futile." The blond vampire said.

All fight stopped immediately and they looked at the blond guy for orders. Jazon said nothing which confused the blond guy.

"You issue no orders to you men?" the blond vamp asked.

Jazon smiled and winked at Ajay and Terry.

"They are my friends; not my minions. They are free to choose their own path, I only intervene for the greater good at times; or give my advice. It is completely up to them if they want to comply or take the advice; I will not force them." Jazon said.

"You could if you wanted though I take it?" blond asked.

"Yes, he could force all of us put together; but he is our leader by deeds and judgment not force. I follow him because he cares if I live or die and will sacrifice himself for me if he thinks I will live. That is the mark of a great man." Terry said.

"Right; he's my boy; we are in it to win it all the way." Ajay added.

The blond vampire's crew picked up the badly damaged among their ranks and carried them out while Jazon and Ajay questioned the blond vamp about Brian, Mark and Collin.

"Do you know where Mark O'Day is? Who is Collin and why did Brian come here to you?" Ajay asked.

SHANE

"Collin is the ruler of all of Europe and he is as far as I know Mark's grand sire. Mark is trash and I would not receive him in my home; therefore, his location is unknown to me. Brain and I are old friends, he is a scoundrel; but I like him anyway. He should have told me about you however. I like not having my home torn up during combat." The blond vampire said.

"I see." Jazon said.

"You must see and speak with Collin soon or he will put hunters on you back. He does not like war being waged in his territories. I will set it up for you as a gesture for not killing my crew and myself; call it professional courtesy." The blond vamp said.

One half hour later they left the blond's home and were off to meet Collin O'Day the lord of the country.

SHANE

SHANE

CHAPTER 2: HOTEL MAGICAL

It was four in the morning and Jax was sitting in the kitchen with Pegi drinking a special tea that Pegi made. It would make an angry bear mellow, and it was very tasty. Jax was not a usual resident of the hotel, but she hung out a lot because Pegi and Tad asked her to help with a lot of organization and logistics. Jax and Pegi totally bonded over the time after Silky was put to sleep. They spent time making sure no one came near the hotel without someone knowing it way ahead of time. Alister made sure that every vamp in the west coast was aware that he would take any attack on the hotel and its people as a personal attack and he would lay siege to those who were guilty. Alister was not a vampire to be messed with; for any reason. It was unbelievable that he was not running the west coast; Alister seemed far stronger in every way that Brian Finney was. Alister simply did not want the hassle was his explanation or the response when the question was put to him by Pegi.

"Are you worried about the boys huny?" Pegi asked.

"Yes and no; I am missing Jazon in my bed, and in my arms. I am afraid I will loose him every time I close my eyes. It dream that he was killed and I was told upon waking up; so I fear sleeping now." Jax confided.

Pegi poured Jax some more tea and then she put her hand over the cup so Jax would not take it. Pegi smiled and pulled a small bottle out of her vest; which had

SHANE

many pockets like a fisherman's vest. The tiny bottle had some lavender fluid in it that seemed to sparkle. Pegi poured some of it into Jax's tea cup.

"Don't ever tell the boys; but I think you deserve to have an extended life. This stuff will keep you young; you will age only one month for every year you live. You are not immortal or invincible; just aging much more slowly. I told Jazon that he should bite you and Ajay and make you like him. Jazon refused because he is afraid you and AJ Rey will turn evil like most vampires and he will have to kill you, or that he could not and you would kill the innocent people out there; which would mean he was responsible. That boy is far to stressed out for his own good, you should help him get over it and bite you." Pegi said.

"I will when he returns; if he does return to me. If some one kills my baby; I am going to make them eat shit and beg before I kill them." Jax said with a sudden rush of ferocity.

Pegi chuckled and took a sip of her homemade hooch. Jax looked at her and smiled.

"I think you could use a drink and some sleep Jax. I would not want to get on your bad side though either way." Pegi laughed.

Tad walked in rubbing his eyes in the bright kitchen lights. Tad had a full head of hair and a long beard to go along with it. Tad did not have on his customary pointed hat; either blue or red.
Tad scratched his head and his butt at the same time.

"Coffee." Tad grunted

"What was that Tad?" Pegi said teasingly.

"Coffeeeeeee!" Tad grunted with one eye closed.

Tad may be six hundred years old; but he was still quite a cute fellow. Just about any human child would want to pick him up and play with him. Tad was not a lite weight though; he was about a hundred fifty pounds of solid muscle under the long hair. Tad gave it away when he did not wear long sleeves; the gnome had bulging arm muscles from working his weapons forge. Tad was also a damn fine wizard or mage, you can choose. His magical ability was pretty elite. If Tad was not a God fearing soul; he could kill you with magic pretty easily; think mini lightning bolts hitting you suddenly; big not good.

"Good morning grumpy." Pegi said.

"I am not grumpy." Tad said.

"Then which dwarf are you?" Pegi asked.

There was complete silence for a moment; and then Jax busted out laughing. Tad looked disgruntle for a brief and then laughed as well.

"Bitch." Tad said to Pegi.

Pegi just kissed his forehead and poured him a huge cup of coffee. When I say coffee; I do not mean that fru

SHANE

fru BS, I mean **Folgers Mountain grown black coffee with six lumps of sugar. Tad sat on the table next to Jax and drank his coffee serenely happy for the moment. Jax had to admit when Tad was around she always felt hopeful about things; she did not know why; she just did. Jax wondered if any one else felt that way or if she was the only one?**

"I have been wanting to make you an offer ms. Jax." Tad said

"You dirty old gnome; her man is away and you start trying to work the girl?" Pegi said in mock exasperation.

Tad ignored her; Pegi and tad sparred verbally all the time because they were close friends; and the most powerful magic users in the hotel.

"I wish to offer you some weapons of your own. I will make them out of Mithril Silver; so they can kill both Werewolves and vampire alike." Tad said.

Jax was speechless; her friends were wolves and other things. Alister was a vampire and so was Jazon; although nothing seemed to work on him. Tad read her mind or expression correctly because he answered her thoughts.

"Lass, not all wolves or vampires are with us child; and I will not see you lost while I have the ability to arm you against a foe; such as those. Jazon would kill me if I let you come to harm." Tad said honestly. "I would not blame him if he did."

SHANE

"You old fool; you know the blades are already made that you want to give her." Pegi giggled.

Tad gave her a shut yer yap look and then looked back to Jax.

"Yes, it is true; I have already made your arms for you; still you have to be asked to accept them." Tad explained.

"I will accept them because I have to and because I would be honored to except any weapon made by the legendary armor Tad Oreilly." Jax said.

"Good, I have them right here with me." Tad said as he snapped his fingers.

The prettiest slightly curves daggers suddenly appeared on the table next to Tad. They had full guards to protect Jax's hands or to punch with. There were runes on the blades and jewels everywhere. These matched blades were likely priceless.

"What do the runes mean Tad?" Jax asked.

Tad smiled and took a great drag on his coffee cup. Lightning quick Tad grabbed a blade and threw it into the wall across the massive kitchen.

"Hey, watch the wall elf!" Pegi shouted.

"Oh shut yer yapper woman. Now, Jax call your blade to your hand; for it will only return to your hand alone." Tad said.

SHANE

Jax held out her hand and then looked at Tad with a question on her lips; she never got to ask it because the blade snapped firmly into her delicate hand. It was lite weight and perfectly balanced. Jax looked over the runes and had another question.

"No." Tad said.

"What?"

"No the runes cannot be removed or used against you. If someone tried to tamper with the blades; they will animate and destroy the guilty party. They are enchanted for you alone. Moreover, you can't be parted from them. If I locked them in the hotel safe and you called for them, they would come to your hands out of thin air girl." Tad explained and took another mouthful of hot java.

"Magnificent." Pegi said.

Tad only smiled and winked at her. Tad was a fine gentleman; he would never leave anything undone if he could help it.

"Ladies today is Sunday, and father Sully will be by in a few hours to read the Lord's word for us. I need to get a few lazy heads up and put them to work setting up the chapel. It was damaged when that trash came into our home. We have been rebuilding it; Block and I; so it should bring a good smile to the Reverend when he comes today; and hopefully our God as well." Tad said with a wink.

SHANE

Tad slipped off the table and landed on his feet without spilling a single drop of coffee. He turned, bowed and then he stomped his way down the hallway to the stairs. Tad never used the elevator; he might have short legs but he liked to use them he would say; so he took the long flights of stair up to the second floor to wake up a few people or creatures if you like. Block the troll was in the back yard; he slept out under the stairs or clouds; after all it is the Pacific Northwest.

Father Mick Sully looked sad and ill when he came to give the word later that morning. Everyone noticed his lack of life and zeal; that he usually displayed everywhere he went. Mick had fallen in love with the residents of the Hotel Magical, they were hungry for the word of God and they were the practice what Mick preached type. Mick realized that the magical creatures were much more friendly and neighborly than regular humans. They had a sense of community and family that was sacred to them. So, when father Mick Sully came in looking lost and sad; everyone was instantly concerned about the man.

"What has happened Mick; to make you look like that?" Wolf asked.

The aging pudgy preacher; looked at them with the most profound look of despair Wolf and Enoch had ever seen on his face.

"I...am being reassigned to another town and church. That is bad; but what is worse is they are sending in a young snotty nosed kid with enough prejudice in him to fill the Columbia river. I don't know what we are going

SHANE

to do. I believed that you are my mission from God; and as such my holy responsibility to help walk with the Lord." Mick said miserably.

"Is there no hope he will warm up to us?" Block asked.

"None." Mick answered.

There was a long and dreadful silence in the new chapel. Mick Sully looked around and his eyes filled with tears. This was his church and these were his flock to lead to God and they had built him the best church any preacher ever had. It was breathtaking in every detail. The reverend cried unashamed. Two of the elves sat down beside him and comforted the man; elves are very good at comfort.

"Wait, I know how to fix this!" Pegi shouted.
Every single being stopped dead and silent in their collective tracks; and stared at the wild hedge-witch that they all fell in love with; because of her beauty, but mostly for her charm and keen mind.

"How do you plan to accomplish that Pegi?" Enoch asked.

"It is simple really; Sully needs to bring his boss here and witness a service and the bunch of us loving God like we do. More, he will see how much we need Sully and how special his job is; what a crucial job he has; trying to keep us monsters under God's influence. We hint that without Sully there might be some bother...if you follow me folks." Pegi said with a flourish.

There were a thousand stunned faces; Sully was among them. They looked around the room at each other and the weight of Pegi's idea sank in. It was so simple, yet completely thorough in the steps and plan. The room erupted in a cheer and the kitchen faeries began to applaud their cook and commander in the kitchen. (The faeries actually did not recognize anyone as their boss, but they aided Pegi out of affection and she was the best cook in the house).

"It is so simple and so brilliant." Jax said.

"NO!"

The room fell completely silent once more and all eyes went to father Sully who was red faced with horror and anger. He had the look at a man who just learned his family had been murdered; which is not a picture I would want in my mind. Sully looked as if he was having a fit. Everyone waited to give him a chance to explain his outburst. Mick looked around and then the fire left his eyes and sadness returned.

"If I bring another holy man; my regional director here; what if he starts a witch hunt and they bring all the narrow minded religious community down on your heads; I will be responsible for deaths on both sides." Mick practically cried.

"Bullshit, we could beat an entire army without hurting any of them. You are just blowing this out of proportion. You will bring your boss here and I will make him

SHANE

understand how important your work is." Pegi said with zeal only Jax, Biz and Wolf had ever seen before.

The rest of the Sunday went on like normal. The congregation gathered; they sang and they prayed. Father Sully gave one hell of a great sermon. There was not a dry eye in the house. Mick could really call upon the spirit of the lord to move the crowd; and not is a TV preacher way; but in an I love you and he loves you and watches over us all way. It was the kind of sermon most preachers never try to give; not that they could not do it mind you; but because a lot of them could not sell it and own the words with such a deep binding devotion; that they fear no reprisal or ridicule. The congregation was moved to tears the entire time. Father Sully was spent both physically and emotionally by the end of the sermon; at the ending prayer his voice was shaky and he looked like he was going to faint. The two elves that were comforting him earlier stood behind him for just such an emergency. He did not faint but he had to sit in the parlor with Jax, Pegi and the elves for a few hours talking and drinking some of Pegi's energy tea; before he could make the journey home. The elves and a wolf followed him to make sure he made it safely; they always did for his protection without his knowledge.

(ONE WEEK LATER IN THE NEW CHAPEL)

Father Sully showed up with his boss the Reverend John Bishop Jr. in tow; they walked into the small office that Block and Tad had built for Mick to keep his private items in. The desk was ancient redwood and the chair was the throne that king Phillip of Spain sat on during his rein. The three tier file drawer was however A modern design. Rev. Bishop looked around and smiled.

"Your flock must love you very much to give you such fine gifts. It is a shame that you are being moved to another town." John said.

"Yes it is. I wanted to talk to you about how truly special this congregation are Sir." Mick said.

"Oh Micky, please with the sir business, we are old friends." John said happily.

The senior pastor did not miss the misery on the face of his friend and was instantly concerned. Mick Sully was a strong man and a great friend and member of their church family. John found Mick to be the best sermon giver he had even known, and Mick has an open mind and a kind heart; so nothing bothers him. But something was bothering him now; deeply.

"John....John this congregation far more special than I could ever explain. I want you to place your hand on my bible and give you solemn promise in God's name that you will not ever reveal what you are to be shown, and if I must leave my flock; that they will be left in peace unless another pastor wants to lead them to salvation." Mick said in complete agony.

The Reverend John Bishop looked at the man he had known for thirty-six years and decided that if he could

SHANE

not trust Mick, than he could not trust anyone. John placed his hand on Mick's golden bound Bible.

"I give my word on this bible in Jesus's name; that I will not ever reveal what I am shown, not by deed or action; so help me God. Amen." John said.

Sully relaxed visibly, but not completely. He got ready for the service and Mick showed John the hidden back door to the podium. Sully opened the door and was immediately met by the two gorgeous elves, one man and one woman. John's breath caught in his throat at their amazing beauty. The elves smiled and inclined their heads in a show of respect. Both elves had very fine crosses around their necks, they were priceless items. The two pastors walked out and Mick showed John to his seat of honor for the service. Father Sully opened the service with a warm heart felt greeting and then a very well thought out opening prayer for acceptance of the lord's plan; and the mission that we all have in his holy name. Then chapel hummed just after than with a hymn that Pastor Bishop had never heard in a language his did not know; however, it was so hauntingly beautiful. The elves moved forward and translated the song for John.

"The words say. Our father who guides us through our day be praised. Our father who loves us and comforts us in our times of need, be praised. Our father who Shepard's us when we are lost, be praised. All praise to our father; king of kings, lord of lords, our GOD, be praised." The elf explained.

SHANE

"Very fine words and the singing is so amazing. I have never heard anything so lovely in my life and I am getting old." John chuckled.

"You are still young, barely past your youth." The elf said.

The pastor misunderstood the elf's meaning; he thought it was a compliment; when it was a statement of fact from a three hundred twelve year old elf warrior priest. Nonetheless, John was wondering why Mick had asked him to swear an oath to God. Sully went on and gave a outstanding sermon about love and fellowship and how that ties into a walk with God; where you are living with the lord's blessings on you. The congregation was riveted John noticed; because John was riveted by the words of his friend; so he looked at the dark chapel and saw that there were no chatters or sleepers in the house. Literally every person was glued to Mick while he led them. Finally, Mick gave his final prayer and thanked everyone for coming and then he shocked John by adding his heart felt introduction.

"Please remain seated for a moment longer. I would like all of you to meet my friend and boss Reverend John Bishop Jr." Mick said

John stood up and smiled and waved.

"It is very nice to meet you folks." John said.
Mick looked nearly when he looked at John; and then he turned and spoke.

SHANE

"Wolf, Biz please turn the house lights on boys; so that John can finally understand why he was asked to swear to our lord." Mick said with a sad voice.

The chapel which was quite large was suddenly as bright as day and the good reverend looked around and was confused. What was he supposed to see here this morning?

"John put you spectacles on please and then take a look around." Mick said.

"Oh silly me." John said and he reached in his pocket.

John pulled out his glasses and put them on.
He looked around and he was deadly silent as he ran his eyes around the chapel focusing on different persons as he went and there was a wide variety because of the nature of this congregation.

"Oh my dear; I see why you asked me to swear now." John said.

The pastor sat down and looked at Mick. Some of the crowd came forward and pulled up chairs. It was obvious that there was to be some discussion now that john knew Mick's secret.
"Okay spill it Micky; I know there has to be a good story here." John said.

"Wait, would anyone like some tea and cookies?" Pegi asked.

SHANE

They all wanted something to eat and drink; so Pegi asked the faeries to prepare some and bring it out if they did not mind. They loved to help, it brought them joy, so they fluttered their wings and shot off to take care of it.

It was maybe twenty minute until the actual talking began; and it was no surprise when the person who began was Pegi. She just takes over in a Hot mother nature way. He sage words cut right to the quick.

"John Bishop, what you see before you is the magical community. We are all God fearing folks and treat each other with love and respect just like it says in the bible. It is normal humans that labeled all of us evil; well that is a load of huey. We don't start wars; we don't kill for land, riches or any other gain. We live in harmony; with the love of God to keep us safe. The question is what are you going to do John?" Pegi asked.

The senior pastor looked at Pegi so young and desirable and was sure she could not possibly understand the position he was now in. He was educated the next instant about how wrong he truly was.
"I am nearly to my two hundred and seventh year of life and I have lived long enough to see the evil that man does to each other, I ran away from the public because I could no longer watch. Jazon came and rooted me out of my stupor and made me want to live again and be vital." Pegi explained.

"How old are you?" John asked.

SHANE

"206 last birthday." Pegi answered.

"Poppycock, you could not be older than thirty at the most." John said in disbelief.

"Enoch toss me that robe please." Pegi said.

The giant scared up black man tossed Pegi a long dark blue robe. Pegi wrapped it around herself and her hand disappeared into the robe. A moment later Pegi was an old woman again. Jax was the only one that new Pegi had to strip off her clothing before the change because they would not fit her in her older persona.

"Well padre, what do you think now? I am a human and elf mixture, I am what you might call an earth spirit, or hedge-witch; which mean that I can use thing from nature to incredible things; like heal wounds or counteract poisons." Pegi said.

"You should see it all before you decide any thing John." Mick said.

"Such as what?" John asked.

"Wolf, Enoch and Biz change and show my boss your other faces." Mick said.

They stepped away from the other people and each took a deep breath and stilled themselves; all at once there were two huge werewolves and a fire demon. The pastor nearly fainted at the sight. John began to say a prayer. Bizerc the fire demon walked over and sat on the top stair near the pulpit and addressed the pastor.

"It is a lot to take in is it not? I am just what you think I am; I am a demon and I am also a recovered soul. I made my plea to God for his divine forgiveness and I was jointed with the boy you saw before I change places with him and emerged. Biz and I are one by the command of God; I protect and walk with him. He was dying when I asked to be forgiven; so I was given the option to be a free demon or to have my soul and the boy's bound together for all eternity, I chose the boy and gave him my strength to recover from his life ending problem. I get forgiveness and the boy became semi immortal." Bizerc explained.

"You are a creature of God?" John asked in a terrified voice.
"Yes, I am one of the fallen. I was a fool and I admitted my sins and asked to be given a chance to earn my way back to heaven and become a regular angel again. I am not in a hurry though; I find that I love the boy who I walk with, we are like brothers; I could not leave him now even for salvation of my own soul." Bizerc said.

    John looked like he was going to die of fright, but he believe in the power of his savior and forged on. The two people who had been with him before and translated the song were not human he now realized; they were immortal elves. He was compelled to ask them a question suddenly.

"Are elves immortal?" John asked.

SHANE

"Yes and no. We can live practically forever if we are not mortally injured or drained of our blood." The male elf answered.

"Why did you say drained? And why do such powerful being need to congregate and worship God? Don't get me wrong folks; I know I will always serve God by why do you?" John asked in a stuttering tone obviously still afraid.

There was a moment of laughter and then Wolf transformed back into a man and quieted the group.

"I am Kalesar; I am three hundred and twelve years old. I am one of a few warrior priests left in the world. I have served God since your people lived huts and caves. As far as blood loss goes; it is usually a vampire that drains our blood away; that is why we stick together; vampires rule the planet John." Kal said smoothly.

"Vampires!" John said in horror.

All the mirth in the room was lost at once. Mick came and sat by john and explained the entire story of how they got here. He explained about Jazon and his vow to God to protect and Ajay's vow to stay by his side and make the world safe for all man and creatures alike. Mick explained that vampires feed on non-humans so that they don't get caught by the human law. Mick Sully talked for a long time and John only listened and did not interrupt him, not even once. When there was no more to explain Mick stopped and drank some tea.

"So, those two young men will take on the world's most powerful predators for the great good? I knew I saw something special in those boys; since they were very young. Jazon is the most dedicated friend you could have, because he does not think about himself, only his goal." John said.

There was a general agreement about Jazon and Ajay being the stuff of legend.
"Wait I have another question. Aren't werewolves supposed to be evil and blood thirsty? I mean no offense; I just need to know." John asked.

"Let me answer this question." A tiny girl said.

"Okay Winky, you can explain for all of us." Wolf said.

The tiny girl bowed to Wolf; which was not missed by the sharp attention John was showing. The girl turned to John and the bigger creatures and people moved out of her way. She stood by Pegi who had turn her body young again and redressed herself.

"First you must know something very important to us; All of us. We never lie; to lie is to kill a part of the world. Mankind lies and cheats and steals; we do not. Lying serves no master except itself, once spoken a lie has a life of its own. Now, wolves hate vampires; some of us have served the enemy because they hold a person precious to your heart hostage to force us to do their evil bidding. We are not evil; when you heard a wolf bay at the moon, it is anguish and sorrow that you hear reverend, now malice and bloodlust. We are a sad and power race, but we can't let a loved one perish no

SHANE

matter the cost to ourselves." Winky explained and then blushed.

"I would like to be introduced to your friend and elder Mick; that is if you don't mind?" A booming deep voice said from the shadows,

A behemoth walked into the light and smiled. The werewolves were big, but they were small next to this creature with green-brown skin. The top of his free dirt colored hair was close to the roof.

"My apologies Block; I did not know you were attending the serve today." Mick said.

"You know I would never miss one of you uplifting sermons father Sully, I just prefer to stay at the window outside for obvious reasons. I know the floor in here can support me so; I can in to meet your guest." Block said.

"How could you know the floor could hold you?" John asked in total awe of the giant troll.

"Why because I laid the floor myself and I built much of what you see, as Tad's partner in the project." Block explained

"I am Tad Oreilly sir." A strong voice said from beside the shocked pastor.

Tad got a pretty good look over before the pastor spoke. John kept looking at Tad and then at Block. He wanted to ask or say something pretty badly. Tad snickered in his odd way and helped the man out.

SHANE

"I am a gnome and Block is an old troll, I am six hundred and some years old and Block is close to that I believe. I am a maker, and no I am not the same kind of maker Jesus was. I make weapons, jewelry and furniture and other items. I am also one of the most powerful magic users alive; Pegi is also extremely powerful in the realm of magic." Tad explained.

The pastor looked at him and shocked Tad by laughing deep and long. Tad drank from his over sized coffee cup that said "NO, I don't sleep in here" and waited for the reverend to recover.

"I am sorry; I am not laughing at you. It is just this is some much to chew on at once. Magic, monsters, you have all changed my entire belief system and preconceived notions about the world I live in. It is the irony that made me laugh; we are so blind to the larger world and the other children of God right now." John said.

"It is a steep learning curve for sure Pastor Bishop; Jazon is my boyfriend." Jax said.

The pastor looked at Mick and then stood up with a stern look on his face that made more than just Mick feel dread coming into their stomachs.

"Pastor Mick Sully also know as Father Sully, you are no longer alone in you struggle to help these people. You will not be transferred. You and I will make sure these folks are helped along with their walk with the lord. I am frankly intrigued by all of this and more than a little scared; however I want to know more about you all, especially the very old among you; you represent living history to me." John announced.

Block reached out and grabbed John which scared the life out of him until the pastor realized that Block was pulling him on his shoulders while the room erupted in cheers. John noticed a distinct apple pie smell; that was very pleasant.

SHANE

CHAPTER 3: ALISTER.

In the dark of night Alister sat in his chair wishing he knew what had become of Jazon and his party. Alister did know that the Bobbies tried to detain them at Heathrow and there was an assassin there to kill Jazon or one of the others no doubt. Alister was worried as well about the werewolves that went with Jazon. Werewolves usually turned on their masters and killed them. In all the world only werewolves was any kind match for a vampire. Strange; that Ajay a human and two werewolves were Jazon's first choice as soldiers; a weakling and two dogs? Jazon was a mystery; Alister had to solve or pay the consequences. Alister called on of his European contacts and inquired about the state and peace of the region. The man told Alister that a group of Yanks busted into the blond vampire's house in London and beat up Ming and nearly killed the blond as well. It was also reported that Brian Finney had been there but escaped with his life into the night.

"My God, that boy is going to start a dark war if he is not careful." Alister said to himself.

Ming was the nephew of Kahn or the Kahn if you would rather. Kahn ruled the Asian continent with a iron grip. Kahn was a small quiet man; but he was not silent. He was old and wise and completely without mercy for his enemies. Why in the world would this young one take shots at one of the two most powerful vampires on the planet? Presently, Jazon was in London which is

SHANE

Collin O'Day's realm; and Collin will not allow anyone to make war in his territories, or hunt there without his consent. Alister was torn between letting the boys get killed and taking over the west coast and the feeling of friendship that he felt for this very unusual young man and his family. Alister was also struggling with his honor; he had given Jazon his word of honor to protect his area and all the inhabitants that dwelled there. Alister and his people were vampires; translation, they needed blood to survive. Jazon could still eat human food and get strong, but he was different from every other vampire on the planet. Alister had decided that he would fly in some convicts from the east coast; who would trade their lives for money for their families. Since they were on death row anyway; they thought this was a good deal. Alister was a kind man at heart so the victims were put to sleep and simply drained of their blood painlessly. Alister did not think that this would break the spirit of his word to Jazon.

"Sir Alister?" a soft voice said.

Alister had been so lost in thought he did not know he was not alone; until he heard his name. Alister was very fast even for a vampire; his inhuman speed had helped him stay alive all these years. Alister was on his feet across the room at an odd angle with a blade in his hand. The man who spoke his name was a small frail looking creature, clearly not human. The fellow had hair but clean feet and was no more than four foot tall. The defining feature of the visitor was his huge sunflower colored eyes. He was a gelfling; a cross between an elf and a dwarf or gnome. A gelf took the good looks of the elves and the smaller size of the dwarf or gnome; they

SHANE

were extremely smart although shy. Gelflings looked frail and delicate but that would be a mistake to believe; they were the children of two very tough races and fast as a blur; add a blade to that equation and you get assassin. Gelflings did not like violence but if pushed they were nearly as dangerous as a werewolf or a vampire.

"Good meet little gelf." Alister said.

"Good meet Sir Alister. I have been asked to invite you to dine with us this evening; if that would be convenient for you?" the gelf said.

"I can think of no reason to not accept the invitation; what time am I to arrive?" Alister asked.

"7:30 pm; just after sundown if that pleases you." The gelf said.

"That is acceptable to me, I will be there. What is you name?" Alister asked.

"Nixander or Nix for short sir." Nix said.

"Good journey Nixander." Alister said.

"Thank you and long life to you Sir Alister." Nix said.

The gelf was gone in a wisp as Alister watched him go. Alister was amused by the small gelf; Alister had always had a soft spot for their kind and he had refused to ever drink on of them. Alister believed they were blessed by God and as such completely off limits as

SHANE

prey, his clan was of a similar notion; so they did not trifle with the gelf when he was moving as a normal human gate.

"Dinner, I wonder what brought this on?" Alister asked himself.

Alister was a business man and had no time to piddle around wondering about anything; so he went to his business and let dinner time come around at its own pace. When Alister's personal assistant advised him it was nearly time to head to the dinner; Alister was shocked that the day had ran by so fast. Megan his assistant; as if she could ready his mind answered his unasked question.

"You did a great deal of business today. I would say I have rarely seen anyone more productive than you." Megan said sweetly.

Megan was one of a few pure humans found inside of Alister's clan and business life. Megan was madly in love with Alister. Megan was tall and had a firm athletic body and bright brown eyes and a lethally sharp mind. Megan never made any bones about the fact she wanted Alister to take a more person interest in her; most men who were not gay or blind; had an interest in Megan. Alister wanted her the same way, but he felt that he would be stealing her youth and life away and she could be killed once she was turned by a hunter trying to get at him. Megan's humanity was her only safety right now with Finney ousted.

"Thank you Megan; and would you like to come to dinner with me this evening?" Alister asked.

Megan smiled at him and then leaned forward and kissed his cheek.

"Yes, I would love to. Let me change into a more suitable dress and then I will collect you so we can leave and be on time." Megan said the last part with a little more emphasis on the last few words.

The smile on Alister's strong features meant he understood her meaning; Alister was always late. Like most vampires; he felt when he got there then that was the right time; because he didn't wear a watch or carry a time piece. Thirty minutes later Megan was in a short sleek black backless dress and mid range pumps. She was lovely as always and Alister wanted to turn her and own her body and soul; but he actually loved her and refused to put her in harms way.

"You look dapper Alister." Megan said with a smile.

Alister was old only in years as a vampire. To the world Alister might be forty tops and a hot forty year old he would be. He was slim and fit; all lean hard muscle. His face was male model good looking; think Sean Connery meets Brad Pitt look. Alister had long silver blond hair and powder blue eyes and a serious smile on his face most of the time; that most people found unsettling. Megan love the way his face looked and she had never feared him. She knew from the beginning he was a vampire and she told him if he wanted to taste her just ask. They had been together every since.

SHANE

"Shall we leave Megan?" Alister asked her.

"Yes, of course; thank you." Megan said sweetly.

Alister ever the gentleman took Megan's hand and walked her to the limo out front of his build and sometimes home.
(AT HOTEL MAGICAL)

Jax and Pegi had taken extra time to put together a fine dinner for Alister and likely his guests. It seemed extremely unlikely that the vampire lord would come without his guards; so Pegi planned to feed them as well. Pat the butcher supplied the hotel with enough raw meat to feed the 1st CAV division of the US Army, and still Pegi and the faeries brought in more food preparation. There was exotic fruit from the market in Vancouver BC and Alaskan King crab. Pegi had been cooking for hours and shouting (lite hearted) orders as she went. The smell of baked goods could be smelled and enjoyed for miles around. It was the opposite of the Camas Pulp mill stank.

Jax had her hands full with the hotel décor and the evening wear for many of the dinner guests. Jax was very good at making clothing both elegant and sexy at the same time. The nymphs, elves and faeries did not need any help looking fine as hell; however there were many others who were a big job to make look good. Block amazed Jax by donning a suit coat as big as a quilt, it was black pin strips and very nice. Jax finally got to dress herself; she put on a red and black mini dress that showed off her sexy figure and great legs;

yet did not look trashy in anyway. Jax looked at Silky lying on the bed; so beautiful and sexy...dying. On a whim, Jax took a dress that looked like her and dress Silky in it. Jax fixed Silky's hair and put little golden earrings in her ears and then she called down the hall for Biz. The handsome young man came immediately.

"I want Silky to sit next to me at dinner, can you get her there and make it so she can sit up stably and at the least listen to us talk. I know she can hear us; she is only deeply asleep." Jax said.

Just to prove that Jax was right Silky had a sudden tear roll down her cheek. Jax and Biz both saw it instantly. Jax held Silky so tight she was hurting herself.

"The boys will catch those dirt bags baby and we will all be here when you wake up; I promise. I am going to make sure you get to go outside during the day and at night; you might be locked inside yourself but your little body can be moved so life does not pass you by. I love you sister." Jax said with a sob.

Biz wrapped his wiry arms around both girls and then silent lifted Silky up and carried her down the stairs to where she would sit for the night; which was on Biz's lap. Biz and Silky were best friends and it was killing the silent boy that his closest friend; other than Bizerc the demon who was with him at all times. Biz had a special link with Silky she could hear his thoughts. Biz stopped and ran back to Jax and scared the hell out of her. He was completely insane with motion; he was

SHANE

trying to tell her something. Biz stopped in a huff of frustration and became Bizerc.

"The kid can hear Silky's thoughts Jax; she is talking to him in his head and visa versa. Silky loves you and she is so glad you finally realized she is in there alone. It might be a pain in the ass, but have Biz get a pad and pencil and write what Silky says so you can talk to her." The demon said.

"OH MY GOD, how could I have been so stupid; Silky is a magical person; of-course she can still communicate!" Jax started crying.

Biz the boy (17 ish, a guess since nobody really knows and he does not age); was once again holding Silky; he reached forward and squeezed Jax's shoulder and smiled. Biz was a very good looking guy. Biz made the writing motion in the air before Jax and she jumped to the small desk by the door and found a pad. Silky had a lot to say and had been listening all the time and even she forgot to reach out to Biz and talk; because she was scared and sad. It was easy; you talked to Biz and Silky; then Biz would write Silky's response, slow but brilliant.

Alister and Megan arrived at exactly 7:30pm on the dot. Wolf and Tad met the vampire at the door and showed him the way to the dining hall. Alister was amazed; the entire inside of the old hotel was all new and it was spectacularly done. Megan who was human and young had never been here before and she was equally impressed.

SHANE

"Your work Tad? Alister asked.

"Some of it is mine; other parts I design the basic idea and then let the folks take a creative license with it. Block did most of the grand wood work since he can ask the wood to obey him; that one is quite the artist. Look up at the ceiling." Tad said.

The group stopped and looked up. The ceiling and supports were all spirals and intricate patterns that were better and more grand than seen any where else ever. Megan gasped at the sight of them.

"How long did it take Block to do that to the ceiling? Megan asked.

"About one week give or take a day or so." A deep booming voice said.

Megan turned around and was looking at the thigh of the biggest person she had ever seen. He was green-brown and smell like hot fresh apple pie. She looked up and realized this was not a man at all.

"Hello down there tiny human, I am Block the troll." Block said with humor in his tone at the face Megan made.

"Do you know that you smell like hot apple pie Block? It is intoxicating you know." Megan said.

Megan stepped forward and offered her tiny hand to block to shake. Block clutched her hand softly between his thumb and index finger and shook it so gently.

SHANE

"Yes little one I have been told. Most trolls smell like fungus, I smell good to humans; go figure?" Block said.

"I thought that since I lived and worked with vampires and a few werewolves that I knew about the magical community...I was wrong." Megan said.

Tad snickered and Block rumbled in his chest; which was him trying to suppress his laughter. Tonight the young woman would get a huge shock and wide variety of new experiences. There was going to be music and singing by the elves and faeries and magic show by Nix and strangely enough Winky who was learning to do some small but visually amazing tricks. Alister was also going to be surprised.

"There is a great and wider circle of beings here tonight that you have only heard of in legend." Tad explained.

Jax appeared and Alister took her offered hand and kissed it. Megan was not the jealous type; but Jax was radiant in her little dress. Jax smiled and then extended a hand to Megan. Megan smiled nicely and shook her hand.

"I am Jax; the girlfriend of Jazon Wild. I am also one of four pure humans here this evening; as are you I believe?" Jax said.

"Yes I am; and I am with Alister." Megan said in a very territorial voice.

Both Pegi who just walked up and Jax busted out laughing at Megan. Tad and Block tried not to but they laughed as well. Megan was confused and a little angry. Pegi explained.

"Huny, there is nothing and no one that could turn Jax's head away from Jazon; they are like to chained souls' not complete without the other. One day when you meet the master of the castle you will understand; so there is no need to be even slightly jealous or protective of Alister' we are not humans here; we play by a more honorable standard here." Pegi said.

Before Megan could answer; Pegi who was dressed in a floral pattern mini dress that showed off her hard body; slide her arm around Megan's waist and towed her into the dining hall; which took the girl's breath away; from the general splendor. Alister, who was holding Megan's hand; was dragged into the room as well and his reaction was no less impressive than Megan's; he was shocked. The room was now sunken four steps down and it was gigantic. There were four stellar light fixtures hanging at perfect intervals and cub lighting along all four walls to provide mode lighting and accents. There was a massive table with several interlocks that held hundreds of different hot dishes and there were matching wine goblets accompanying the dishes. Seated at all but a few of the chairs was the most fantastic collection of mythical beings the world had ever known. Every one of the creatures stood up or the equivalent when Pegi and Jax walked in with Alister.

"Oh my." Alister said.

SHANE

"Welcome Sir Alister!" the room said in unison.

Megan was way passed shock at the folks in the room. There were giants, ogres, faeries, pixies, a unicorn, some goblins, a mermaid in a giant bowl; and a small yellow dragon in the far corner. There were also many dwarves, elves, gelfling and some other creatures that were not well known.

"Are we in any danger? " Megan asked honestly. "Oh God, I do not mean any offense."

"No offense taken little one; you are in no danger at all; most of what humans are told about us is horse shit." Tad said huffily.

"Be that as it may; please come in and be seated; so that we get dinner under way. I would like for you to sit with our other special guests at the other end of the table." Jax said in her manager voice.

"By the dragon?" Megan said in fear.

(Snicker)

"Yes miss by me." said the dragon from across the room.

Megan did not say anything she just had a death grip on Alister's arm. Alister believed that he was put by the dragon just in case he attacked anyone; a dragon was much too much for a vampire to deal with alone or even in force. Nonetheless, Alister sat where he was bid and made no outward sign he was nervous. Pegi walked to the head of the table and Enoch stood beside her.

"Welcome everyone; and thanks for coming. You were not seated willy-nilly; but according to the food that I personally prepared for each of you. So if you don't like the dinner, tough shit; you can cook next time. Thank you." Pegi said with a chuckle.

The room erupted in a riot of laughter; even Alister laughed good heartedly. Pegi looked around and smiled; she was once again so happy that Jazon and Ajay got her off her old butt and back to living a life.

"Was the last part of the speech for me Pegi?" Alister asked.

"No the middle part was." Pegi answered.

"That would be...?" Alister asked.

"Lift up the top off the platter in front of you Alister and take a look." Pegi said.

The vampire did just that and found very fresh steak tar-tar, and that was still warm.

"Oh now I understand, you seated me here because this is where the food that was prepared for me is located." Alister said.

"True and because the kitchen is behind the door to your left; it made getting a fresh killed meat on your platter while fresh a bit easier for me and Pegi. Try the

SHANE

wine as well; you will find it to your liking I think. It is Jazon's creation." Jax said.

Alister poured himself a glass of wine and took a sip. He smiled and looked at the glass when he pulled it away from his mouth. Megan was not sure what the look on Alister's face was; she thought he might have been drugged or poisoned until he spoke.

"This is a strangely appealing wine. It is a dessert wine with blood added to it is it not. The blood is not human blood but I can't place it?" Alister said.

"It is the filtered blood of cows and pigs. Jazon and a local butcher perfected the process. The blood is cleaned of any impurities and remains whole with nothing floating in it' if you know what I mean." Wolf said. "Jazon will not drink human blood; he is not even tempted. Therefore, he found away around his biological need for blood. What do you think of his solution?"

The silver-blond vampire smiled and took another sip of the wine in a dignified way and then cleared his throat.

"I am honestly impressed; I am not surprised though. Nothing that young man does surprises me over much. Jazon and his shadow are the two most interesting men I have met in two hundred years. They have brought peace to this region; proof of that sits around this great table this evening." Alister said.

Movement behind Alister made him snap to his feet. Wolf was right beside him with suddenly black eyes.

SHANE

The yellow dragon and had gotten up and took a step toward the table; it looked at Alister with no real concern and leaned passed him and put his massive head next to Megan's.

"Pardon me lovely maiden; but do you think you could help me gather my dinner and bring it over to my table. Sadly I am embarrassed to admit this but having no hands I am at a disadvantage." The yellow dragon said in a soft tenor voice.

The entire room was shocked; no creature had even heard the dragon speak before. Megan went from terrified to amazingly interested. She got up really slow and looked at the dragon; who made a small closed mouth grin; trying to hide his huge teeth from the human.

"Which dishes are for you?" Megan asked.

"Those five giant platters there in the middle; I can eat them where they are; however it would make a mess for anyone below me. I would never be so rude to so beautiful a lady." The dragon said.

"I would be glad to assist you but I fear I am too weak to lift even one of those platters." Megan explained.

"Yes, I can see you are quite a petite girl and so lovely; I am sure you could get some of the wolf pack to help you bring those over to my round table." The yellow dragon said.

SHANE

The wolf pack looked at Wolf and he winked at them. Four muscular young men stepped forward and made a slight bow and then lifted the platters that had whole hogs and sides of beef on them quite easily and walked over and placed them on the table. When the five platters were in place Megan herself opened the lids and served the dragon with a smile.

"Thank all of you and especially you kind lady. Now please step way back; I am going to heat my food and I would simple die if I burnt you by accident." The yellow dragon said.

Megan walked back to Alister's side and the small yellow dragon made a short inhale and then shot a small jet of flame out over the table. The smell of flame broiled pork and beef was intoxicating. The yellow dragon tested the beef with his forked tongue and then he shot a smaller flame out his mouth for a twenty count and then he looked at Megan.

"My lady would you care for some freshly cook meat before I dine?" the dragon asked.

"Yes please; a little of both would be nice." Megan said.

Megan took her plate a knife and a fork and walked over and carved two very nice steaks of the cooked meats; one pork steak and one beef. Megan touched the yellow dragon on the end of his nose affectionately.

"What is your name?" Megan asked.

"I have no name in a human tongue or any language that is non-dragon." The yellow dragon said.

"Would you allow me to offer a nick name?" Megan asked.

The yellow dragon that was small; by dragon standards was still bigger than an elephant; raised his head up and looked down at her from way above. Slowly like he was unsure of his own mind the dragon looked away and then dropped his head down.

"What nick name would you suggest?" the dragon asked.

"Well you are yellow so how about, lemon or banana? No wait I think I sunrise is more like it; because that is what you scales look like to me." Megan said.

"Well, I am not into fruits as a moniker; however, Sunrise appeals to me. It is powerful and subtle at the same time; I accept this name you have offered." Sunrise said.

Alister took a deep breath and turned around and looked across the table at two men sitting there looking back at him. Alister was about to go around the table and question them when Enoch was behind him.

"May I get you anything Alister, or are you ready to sit and dine?" Enoch said in a deep voice.

SHANE

"I am well take care of already thank you." Alister said as he sat down next to Megan who had just been seated.

The vampire continued to stare at the two men. Jax was starting to think the night might not go as smooth as they hoped. The men were looking as hard at Alister as he was at them. Finally, it came to a head.

"Are those holy men; because I can swell holy water on them and velum?" Alister asked, in an angry voice.

"Yes, we are; but don't be offended by us; we are here as friends of the family; the entire family. You are however; the first true vampire we have ever met and we are intrigued by your eloquence and courtly nature." Mick said.

"I see; so you are not here to start some kind of witch hunt for vampire then?" Alister said.

The two pastor's looked at each other and then at Pegi.

"Most definitely not; Pegi is a witch and we could never let any harm come to her. More, I see no reason to pit the church at least ours against you or anyone else...as long as you are no threat to us." John explained.

"Do you wish me to believe that you can look at all of us and not find fault in our very existence?" Alister asked.

"I have been the pastor of this big family for sometime; Jazon brought me in and asked me to lead these folks in the worship of the lord; and I accepted the calling and have been doing my very best to keep them safe and secret for the eyes of man...especially the narrow minded among the church and government." Mick said.

"Hmmm...I am not a regular vampire either, I don't drink mankind by choice, none of my clan do. We are an old family and a powerful one, but we are not Jazon who walks in the sun; and we are not the blight that preys on humans either. I am somewhere in the middle of those two extremes. I want peace, but will kill to defend what is mine." Alister said in a harsh way.

"It is still a pleasure and a privilege to meet you; we are fascinated by all of the wonders that our association has brought us. I and we offer you no threat of danger or opposition in any form; moreover, your very existence is safe with us because we can not divulge the truth about any of them either. That literally puts us in the loose ally category don't you think?" John said.

The silver haired vampire looked at the pastors and smiled. Here were two men worth his time, they had courage and intelligence. Alister finally understood why he was here; Alister was invited to see the amount and variety of the alliance that was behind Jazon's hotel. More, he was invited here to see that the group was expanding their friendships into the most unlikely place the church itself; which for centuries had hunted and tried to kill all of them. Times had truly change Alister thought to himself.

SHANE

"Let us drink to friendship ladies and gentlemen and enjoy the bounty Pegi and her staff have prepared for us all." Alister said.

The entire banquet room toasted to friendship and then dined like royalty and enjoyed the company of old friends and new.

CHAPTER 4: THE THEFT

In a small hamlet in the Glen Fininen area of Ireland the IRA were having a meeting about the civil disobedience they were planning over the rough handling of one of there children; The plan was completely non-violent; although perhaps it should have been; after all they police hurt a child. A young man; who was just past his childhood since his parents were killed a year and some months ago, stood and listened. The IRA was used to the young man being around, he was not one of them; however he did them favors sometimes. The favors were jobs actually; theft mostly and deliveries. This was one of those times. In addition to the civil disobedience; they also wanted to have something stolen from the royal police tower in Dublin and since it was heavily guarded and fraught with alarms; they needed a thief who would be able to get by all of that and score. Connor was their man; he was fifteen years old and mean as an Adder. He spoke rarely and when he did it was worth hearing; likely it was a warning to back off. Connor had an affinity with knives, as in he could palm one and slit your throat in a blink and conceal the blade in one deft movement.

"So Connor we have a job for you; one that pays well lad." The head of the cell said.

"What is it you have for me boys?" Connor asked.

"The royal pains in me arse; stole the ring of the last Good King Finn's kin. It is a ring that mean as much to

SHANE

the people of Ireland as it does the Irish parliament. We want you to good and steal it back for us; it is no easy one lad; but we have no other way to get is back. Will you give it a try?" The leader asked.

Connor was 5'8 and 145lbs and he had the wild eyes of a man much older than him. He stared down the IRA cell and asked the obvious question.

"How much?" Connor asked.

"Well we were thinking about five hundred pounds sterling." The leader said.

"Let me get this right; I am going to steal a priceless ring; brave the royal police and all their bloody alarms and the offer for life in prison is; for five hundred sterling?" Connor said.

The IRA cell was quiet to the person; Connor had spoken the truth and was waiting for their honest answer. It seemed that they were asking a lot of him for very little in the way of pay. I voice behind them spoke and startled everyone.
"I will pay you one hundred thousand pounds sterling if you take the job. That ring needs to stay in Ireland where it bloody belongs." said the well dress man.

On of the IRA was about to pull his pistol when Connor noticed and placed his hand quickly over the man's hand. The man looked at Connor; and saw the fear in Connor's fearless face and then decide not to pull his weapon on the new comer yet. The nicely dressed man noticed the exchange and smiled.

SHANE

"You are very wise for one so young." The man said.

"Caution and prudence have kept me alive...vampire." Connor said.

"WHAT?" the IRA gasped in unison.

The vampire smiled and nodded that it was true; he did not however take his eyes off Connor. The young man barely blinked and his every muscle was as taut as spring steel ready to strike.

"You know me then young man?" The vampire asked.

"No, I don't know you personally; but I know your kind." Connor answered.

"How is that young man?" the vampire asked.

Connor made a minute movement and twin knives slide into his power hands.

"A vampire killed my family and drank them dry, he left me alive by mistake and I have been searching for him every since." Connor said in anger.

The human boy's eyes were narrow and deathly cold; it was obvious he intended on killing the vampire. That factoid was not lost on the vampire; who was as old as Ireland nearly.

"I offer my heart felt apology for your loss; however if you try to stick either one of those blades in me son; I

SHANE

am going to give you a good thrashing." The vampire said.

"You're welcome to try...mate." Connor said as he went into motion.

The young man was faster and more skilled than any of the IRA could have imagined. Connor managed to put both silver blades into the vampire's chest and was still moving with a new set of deadly blades in his hand. The vampire was grimacing because silver is poison to vampires. Connor never slowed down to gloat, he moved like a pack of wolves trying to take a bear down. Connor put three more knives into the vampires back before the vampire stopped his assault. The vampire pulled the blades free and tossed them in front of Connor and in a blur of movement had a sword in his hand and it was at Connor's throat.

"Okay you have me; go ahead finish it. Take my life; I have nothing left to live for anyway." Connor snarled at the vampire.

The vampire looked at the young man; he focused on the eyes. The young man had no fear at all none. The vampire listened to the boy's heart it was not even beating hard; it sounded like he was asleep; and all of this with a razor sharp sword at his throat; amazing.

"I do not seek your life or the life of any human. More, I am not in the habit of killing or watch brave men killed for no reason. You have a great strength in you; it should be cultivated not destroyed. Do you know who I am?" the vamire asked.

SHANE

"You are a blood drinker; what more do I need to know about you?" Connor said in a calm voice.

The vampire surprised Connor and the IRA cell by laughing and sheathing his sword; and then he stepped forward and offered his hand to shake to Connor.

"I am Collin O'Day."

Two things happened at once; the IRA were dropped to their knees and looked at the ground while shaking in blind fear; and Connor slapped the hand away. Collin smiled and offered the hand again. Connor just looked Collin in the eye.

"I will not let a man who could put five blades in me die. I rule over all of Europe young man; kings and government grovel at my feet and yet you stare me down like a common thug. I like that about you. Lets you and I make medicine as my American Indian friend would say; I will help you track down the vampire who killed your family and send them to their reward and you get me that ring and come learn to use a sword from me." Collin said.

Connor thought about it for a minute; he even turned his back on Collin while he did; the IRA thought this was rude and feared for Connor's life. Collin saw the gesture as a sign of respect; Connor was showing that he felt Collin had enough honor not to attack him from behind. Collin knew the young man was not relaxed and he would instantly fight if attack and give a very fine

SHANE

account of himself. Connor made up his mind and faced Collin.

"Deal; you help me find and kill the one I seek and I will stay and learn the sword from you. Be aware I am no man's slave or stooge and I will not be treated like one. I will also retrieve the ring as requested. If I get caught; then our deal is off I guess." Connor said as he offered his hand to Collin.

The vampire lord and thief shook hands like gentlemen. Collin led Connor to his 1946 Bentley; where Amus was waiting with the door open. Connor gave the older man a sniff and was surprised when he was found to be a pure human and not a blood drinker. Connor was confused and Amus could see it plainly on the young man's face.

"My family has had the privilege to serve the house of O'Day for generations. Master Collin is as much my friend as he is my employer; I would not hesitate to do anything in my power to serve or protect him." Amus Savage explained.

Collin put his hand on Amus's shoulder and gave a gentle squeeze. They were friends as unlikely as that seemed. Connor was not ready to believe this little factoid, it seemed so against nature. Collin seemed to be able to read minds; because he addressed Connor's thoughts.

"Amus is the great grandson of the first human who came to live and work at my house. Patrick was the first. His family was very poor and starving; so they sold

SHANE

me Patrick to save the rest of the family. I was appalled by this action; however Patrick was a mean child and a burden on his family; so they believed they could fix two issues with one sale. (chuckle) They thought I was going to eat him; actually so did the lad. Patrick was only ten years old when he came to my home. I told him I would eat him tomorrow; but today I want you to dine with me and learn to read and write; for this I will pay you in silver; IF you do as I say. I told him there would be no fighting, swearing or stealing while in my house. Patrick was a strong boy; both in mind and body; he saw a very different life dangling before him and decided to step in to that life and make the most of it. For the next ten years I told Pat; tomorrow I will eat you but today we have work to do. Patrick's family was scared when he went to their little farm with a huge wagon; they were behind on their bills and thought he was there to take everything they had in payment. They were wrong; Patrick went back to say he was sorry and to thank them for selling him to the lord O'Day's estate; because it was the beginning of a new better life for him. Patrick walked into their kitchen and looked at his father, mother, and three little sisters. He smiled and told them that he had paid all their debts off; and then pulled his dad out to the wagon which was filled with pigs and supplies. Patrick's family did not know who he was for hours; until his youngest sister who was eleven came and held his hand and asked why he would do these things for a complete stranger family? Patrick laughed and picked her up and put her on his lap and said, "Baby sister you are not strangers to me". The girl looked hard at him and then gasped.

"You're Patrick my brother?" the girl said.

SHANE

"Yes, honey I am your big brother and I have come home to visit and make sure you are cared for. None of you will ever know hunger again or poverty. I wish for you to prosper and help your neighbors as well. This is the lessons that Collin has taught me; to help you helps me become a better man. Beside I have not seen you since you were a wee baby; or the rest of my family in ten years." Patrick told them.

Patrick's mother who was poor of sight came up close to him and touched his face and looked into his eyes and began to cry.

"I thought we sold you to your doom; I have been so ashamed all these years; with thoughts that you were killed and eaten so that we might live." Pat's mother cried.

Patrick comforted his mother and shook his father's hand firmly. Patrick held and hugged all three sisters lovingly and then he explained.

"When I was sold to Collin; I thought I was dead. Collin was so powerful and so clever; I was sure he was just messing with my mind before he killed me. I was wrong completely. Where I expected death; he offered me a new life; one with education and skills and riches. I work for Collin now; I am not his property. He tried to pay me for my toils; however I refused any compensation until the money he paid for me was paid back to him. I wanted to be a free man. Collin accepted my terms and nearly three years later he gave me a bag of silver coins; this time he made me take them. Collin explained that the money that I had cost him was paid back many times over and this bag of coins was my share form the crops that were sold and the cattle that I had herded to market for him. Collin has been my teacher and my friend for the last ten years, and I am hopelessly dedicated to him. I will not ever leave his side; except to visit you here. Further, my sisters are welcome to come and stay with me and be educated as well." Patrick explained.

When Patrick left to return to Collin's side in the castle and fortress only his youngest sister would go; the other two were scared of Collin who was the most powerful vampire alive. In Ireland it was a death sentence to kill one of Collin's people, which was every single person in the island. Collin did not drink peoples blood, he drank animal blood but only when the animals were butchered for the meat, not just because he wanted blood. Patrick's sister's name was Elaura and she loved her brother with all her heart. She was not afraid of Collin when they met; she held out her hand and declared herself. Collin laughed and shook her tiny hand and then took a knee and bowed before kissing her hand.

"A fine lady your will make little one. I will make sure you are given the best of everything; clothing and education." Collin said.

"I only require a chance to be of use like my big brother; nothing more." Elaura said firmly.

Collin looked at his friend and smiled.

SHANE

"How like you she is my friend. Elaura; your brother was sold to me and I made him a man among men; because it made me happy to see him grow and prosper. I want to give you the same opportunities that I afforded your brother; you payment is you success to me." Collin said.

"I agree to your terms sir." Elaura said hold out her tiny petite hand to shake.

Collin shook her hand and they began a friendship that lasted one hundred ninety-seven years. Collin slipped his blood in hers and Patrick's wine to keep them young and strong for several human life times. The truth was that Collin could not bear to be without them; he loved them like his own children; so he did all he could to keep them alive. Elaura never married because she never found a man who could match up to either her brother or Collin as a person. Patrick did marry and had four boys; all of them chose to stay and work for Collin's estate when they reached manhood. Through the years it became a family tradition to work for the O'Day estate; although every person was free to leave and seek their fortune elsewhere. A few of the children through the years did this; those who returned were welcomed back. However, some died in the wars and were mourned by all.

"Connor what do you think of me now; after hearing the brief history of Amus's family and mine?" Collin asked.

"I am frankly skeptical because you are a vampire and so that makes you evil." Connor said.

SHANE

Amus who was driving slammed on the brakes and looked over the seat at Connor with a hard look on his face.

"Look laddie buck, Master Collin is not like the low level trash that you're used to dealing with; he is a gentleman and you would do well to keep a civil tongue in your mouth." Amus said.

"Just because you're an old fart don't except me to take any shit off of you or anyone else." Connor said in a flat hard tone.

"A yank told me this once; respect is earned not bestowed and so it is: however the inverse is also correct boy." Amus said.

"Yes, I liked that yank; he was a smart mouth; but a keen mind." Collin said.

Connor looked at Collin and then at Amus quietly for a moment and then he broke the silence.

"I will reserve judgment about you for now; please understand that Amus's sycophant persona is not helping me see you as anything more than a common vampire who messed with a human's mind." Connor said.

Amus was about to launch in to another tirade; but Collin held up and hand and smiled.

"It is okay Amus; he is right not to trust me or you; we are unknown quantities and he has survived by his guts

SHANE

and his wits for a long time. I would not expect a slayer to drop his guard even for a moment." Collin said.

The Bentley zipped along at a nice soft pace until they came to a hotel in Dublin. Connor did a double take; he was shocked that they were in the city where he was supposed to steal back a ring. Connor had agreed to do the job; however he did not think it would be tonight. Collin seemed to be enjoying the discomfort of Connor and the look of complete disbelief. Amus brought the car around and parked. Collin got out and he motioned for Connor to follow him. They walked into the ultra exclusive hotel; translation expensive. Collin led the way passed the security; who looked over Connor but made no move to stop him. The manager looked at Collin and smiled; and then he looked at Connor and grimaced.

"The servant's entrance in the rear of the hotel is your man wants to bring in your luggage Sir Collin." The man said.

Connor already had a knife in the palm of his hand; when Collin reach out like chained lightning and slapped the manager across the right side of his face.

"How dare you insult my family?" Collin said loudly.

Connor replaced his knife and watched Collin work the room. The manager had some blood on his lip and he stood in front of Collin trying to find the right words to say to salvage this encounter. Collin never let him speak.

"My nephew has had some rough road lately and is long overdue so R and R; and this is how he is treated because he is not wearing a $5000 suit; SNOB, TRASH, DISRESPECTOR!" Collin yelled at him.

Connor tried not to laugh at the spectacle. Collin had these people in the palm of his hand and Connor realized he just learned his first lesson from Collin; never let your opponent have the higher ground in any way.

"My fervent apologies to your family Sir Collin; we did not know that your nephew was traveling with you. If there is any way we can make it up to you and your family; do not hesitate to ask." The manager said.

"I just want to take a shower and sleep Uncle Collin; so a room would be nice." Connor said as he played along.

"Oh yes sir; it is on the house sir; my compliments and my gift to you for the misunderstanding." The manager said.

The manager missed the look Collin gave Connor as they accepted the room pass card and went to the elevator. Collin stopped and looked at the manager.

"Remember my nephew's face; he is to be treated as royalty at all times; sadly he does not share my flare for attire; so that will not help you identify him." Collin said.

The manager looked ill but made a short bow. Collin gave a look of satisfaction and went into the lift with Connor. When the door closed and the lift began Connor

SHANE

busted out laughing and he looked at the handsome face of Collin and began to laugh like an idiot.

"You are too must governor; the look on that man's face was priceless." Connor said.
"Yes, I suppose it was; I hate pompous snobs; he is not better than you or anyone else." Collin said obviously still irritated.

"Wait does he know what you are?" Connor asked.

Collin looked at Connor and smiled.

"Certainly not; I am a direct descendant of kings and queens. Ireland is mine by birthright; however, I believe in free will, so I govern form the shadows; even though the official government would not think to question my authority." Collin explained.

"What if they did?" Connor asked.

Collin turned his eyes to Connor and there was a inner crimson glow and his teeth were longer and stronger looking.

"I would remove them from the office from which they sit." Collin said plainly.

For the first time Connor was actually nervous standing near Collin. The change in him was absolute and instantaneous. Collin noticed the stress in Connor and let it go.

SHANE

"I take it that you have had to remove someone before? Connor said.

Both men knew it was not really a question; they walked down the 3rd floor hallway toward the suite that Connor would be staying at. When they reached the door; Collin took a deep breath as to calm himself and spoke.

"Yes."

Connor understood that this was the answer to his earlier question and he decided it was better to let the topic go for now. Collin appeared to have something in his craw that was stuck there and he really did not want to talk about it. Connor opened the door and they entered the room. Collin walked right to the window and beckoned Connor over to see. Connor looked out the window and found that they were right next to the royal police tower.

"You are scary sometimes Collin." Connor said.

Collin did not speak and just turned to the door and it was knocked on. The vampire walked across the room and opened the door. Amus was standing there holding a suitcase that looked quite heavy; because Amus was a stout brawny fellow despite his age. Amus walked right in and tossed the case up on the bed and then rechecked the door to make sure it was closed properly.

"Go on and open the case Connor." Amus said.

Connor did open the case and it had everything and then some; for the complete burglar. Connor smiled and took the items out that he knew he would need. Collin gave Connor a box with a black Kevlar suit in it. Connor put that on and loaded up the tools he liked to use when he worked. When Connor was ready; he turned to Collin and asked a question.

"Where is the ring; what floor I mean?" Connor asked.

"From where we stand it is on the 3rd floor and second door from the elevator going west; which is straight away from where we are." Amus said.

Connor narrowed his eyes at Amus. Amus snickered.

"Sir Collin O'Day was given the royal tour and showed the damn ring like they didn't know it was his to take." Amus said.

Connor smiled and chuckled; then shook his head at the ignorance of some people. He looked at Collin and then opened the window and was lost into the night.

(INSIDE THE POLICE TOWER)

Connor went in through the vent on the side of the building; he just cut the wires to the fan and let it noiselessly stop. He crawled inside the air duct and slide softly down into the ceiling of the 3rd floor. The guard walked under him. Connor waited until he passed and then open the vent cover and dropped down silently like a ninja and tapped the guard on the shoulder. When the startled man turned the black figure sprayed knockout mist in his face and he hit the floor asleep; he would stay asleep for twenty to thirty minutes only; so Connor got a move on. Since it was late and the halls were dim, a man in a black body suit makes you hard to see. Connor reached the second door passed the elevator and opened the door with caution. It was empty except for a glass-steel box containing the prize that he was looking for. Connor took out a bottle and filled the room with instanta-fog. Sure enough the room was filled with lasers. Connor brought a mini laser of his own; only his was not a light beam; it was a boring tool. Connor burned a whole through the glass case and shot a mini hook through that hole with a mini crossbow. The hook caught the ring just as Connor planned and he snapped his wrist and the ring shot across the gap right into his hand. Then the alarm went off.

"Damn it, the pad must have been weight sensitive under the ring." Connor growled to himself.

All hell broke loose a second later. Steel bars dropped from the ceiling the entrance of the room. Connor launched himself backwards at a amazing speed and just barely missed having the bar pin him to the floor. That was only one problem. Guards were poring into the hallways. Connor looked down the hall to where he needed to be to get the hell out of here; it was filled with police commandos. Connor grabbed a smoke grenade off his vest and popped the pin and tossed it down the hall way; the police were ready for that. Connor smiled as he ran up the wall around and by the police and then threw two hands full of marble on the floor; when the police turned to pursue Connor thy stepped on the marble and fell flat on their asses as

SHANE

Connor disappeared into the smoke. The police fire blindly into the smoke; they heard a grunt but when the smoke cleared there was only blood and no body.

"Where did that guy go?" one of the police asked.

It was only three minutes later that Connor crawled through the window where Amus and Collin was. The kid was breathing hard and had rails in his breaths.

"Here is your F...ing ring mate?" Connor rasped.

Amus had heard enough guff out of the lad and was about to give him a tap on the chin to teach him a lesson. Connor saw him move and had knives in both hands instantly; but all time stopped as Connor through up blood all over the floor and then he looked up and smiled at Collin and fell flat on his face.

"Oh Jesus Christ help us; the lad has been shot in the back." Amus said as he ripped the comforter off the bed and wrapped Connor in it.

"Go get the car Amus, I will bring our young friend to you; we need to hurry he is bleed a lot." Collin said.

Amus did not have to be told twice; he ran out the door and down the stairs; he left the elevator alone. Collin heard the sound of the Bentley coming to life forty five seconds later. Amus was very efficient; he took pride in everything he did. He was not as funny as his father and grand sire were; but all in all he was a good man and loyal friend. Collin heard the car pull up just under the roof below the windows at the end of the hallway outside of the private suite. Collin picked up Connor who was asleep; and went to the window and jumped to the ground from the 3rd floor; he placed Connor gently in the rear of the car and climbed in just before Amus dropped the hammer and they turned for the road to Collin's home.

SHANE

SHANE

CHAPTER FIVE: O'DAY CASTLE

Jazon was asleep on the train that they decided to take; why they kept changing transportation types was beyond him, planes, trains, automobiles. Jazon was beyond tired; even with his immortal strength; he had been way too long without rest; and he hated to admit it but he was going to need blood soon or because a seriously mean bastard. Ajay noticed the red blood shot ring inside of his friend's eyes and was worried about what he could do about it. Jazon had never let himself get low on blood, he just took a trip to the fridge and had some animal blood and he was good to go for awhile.

"Hey boss; your blood sucker is getting all peckish." Payton said with a tremor of fear.

"Best keep away from him then; and I would keep from being to rude; he might take it personally when he is in this state." Jc said.

Both wolves laughed and nudged the boy; which startled him. Payton liked the rascals; however the black guy and the vampire made him nervous. Jazon looked at him and spoke.

"I am less of a danger to you than the wolves are; because I think about what I am doing before I just loose it and act." Jazon said as his mouth watered.

"Bull; you want to eat me right now." Payton barked.

SHANE

(Weak laugh)

"Little P, I am starving and yes I need blood pretty bad; however, I DO NOT drink human blood ever. Now, you going to share the candy bar in your pocket or not?" Jazon said with a sharp toothed smile.

"Oh man; you were drooling over my candy?" Payton asked.

"Yah, the boss has a wicked sweet tooth bro." Terry chuckled. "Better share man, he is a real beast if he don't get his fix."

   The kid looked at them and was trying to decide if they were messing with him or not. Ajay broke the silence by tossing a sugar daddy sucker to Jazon; who ripped it open and jammed it into his mouth. Jazon grinned and lay back down and closed his eyes; he was asleep almost instantly. Ajay smiled for a second at his weird friend and then watched out the window again. Payton noticed that he had a death grip on his gun and he rarely blinked. It would be a sad day when you crossed that brother's path; Payton was suddenly very happy to be on their side; what ever that meant.

"Hey I am going to go to the dining car, you boy want me to get you anything?" Jc said.

"Raw steak, very bloody please, uncooked." Jazon said without moving his lips. "Feed the boy as well, he looks more than half starved to death and wash him up as well; kinda stinks a bit."

SHANE

"How about you Shadow?' Jc said.

"Naw; I am good man." Ajay said without looking.

(cleared throat)

"Chicken; fried if they got it, baked if they don't." Ajay said looking at Jazon.

Terry did not say anything; he could tell that these two men were so close they could answer each other's sentences and they cared about their friendship deeply. Ajay was only eating because Jazon wanted him too. More Ajay carried candy for his friend; that is what friendship should be like. Terry wanted to build a friendship like that; have a friend that would never let anything come between them; not even fear of death. Terry was so lost in thought he did not hear Jc holler at him.

"Terry you coming or what?" Jc asked.

"No, I gotta look after these guys." Terry said.

"Go eat buddy, you can't hunt around here; so you're going to have to eat strictly human food to keep you strong; and I need you to be healthy and strong kid." Jazon said.

Terry got up and followed Jc and Payton out into the train causeway; and on to the food car. The wolves could smell the food already and it smelled good. They could also smell Payton and he smelled bad. They were

SHANE

going to have to help the kid out and get him cleaned up and into new clean clothes. The dining car was nearly empty save for the crew on duty. The crew perked up when they came in and smiled; they were obviously bored to tears.

"What can we get for you gentlemen?" The burly waiter asked.

"Meat; that is our desire; lots and lots of meat." Jc said with a smile.

"Yes sir; we have plenty of options for your dining pleasure this evening." The man said.

"Start bringing them to that table there." Terry said pointing at a big round one.

The trio sat down around the table and looked at the confused staff. Terry looked at Jc.

"Hey didn't you just say to bring the meat, all of it; then why are they looking at us like we are zombies?" Terry asked.

"Sir; that is a lot of food." The waiter said.

"Yes it is: we are huge eaters. We will however let you know when we are close to done so we don't waste anything; we don't like waste." Jc said flatly.

The staff smiled at them and went to work. They set the table with bread and warm creamy butter. They put pitchers of water and Rootbeer on the table as well as a damn good ale. The trio ate slowly and carefully. They had steaks and ham placed in front of them. Terry took the entire ham and put it on his plate; he sliced off a good portion and gave it to Payton. Jc grabbed the steak platter and did much the same. Within a ten minute period the meat was gone and the boys were looking; well frankly they still looked hungry.

"Excuse me sir; may I see a dessert menu?" Payton asked.

"Certainly young sir; it is right here." The burly man said.

Payton told the menu and looked it over and then he showed it to Terry and Jc. They hummed here and there until they decided what they felt like.

"We will have two apple pies; hot and one banana cream pie for our young friend." Terry said.

"Just to make sure I am not mistaken; you want three full pies?" The burly waiter asked.

"Yes."

"Very good coming up right away." The waiter said.

The staff was in awe of the amount of food the men could eat; and the boy was eating like he had a black hole inside of him. Per their earlier words they did not waste anything and stopped the flow of food before they were finished eating. Jc drank the last of the ale

SHANE

while Terry and Payton worked over the soda. Jc stood up and stretched and then he addressed the staff.

"Before we retire for the night I need so food to go for our friends who did not feel like coming down here tonight. I need one seriously bloody; uncooked steak to go and some fried chicken and four bottles of chilled beer or ale." Jc asked.

"Okay; just give us ten minutes and we will have it all ready for you. Now; how would you like to settle the bill?" the waiter asked.

"The bill; I thought that was part of the train ride?" Jc said.

The head waiter's face began to turn red and he was puffing up; but the rest of the staff was giggling. The burly man looked at them and saw that they were looking back at the table. Jc and Terry were each holding NOTS (rolls of bills, usually a lot of money) and they were tapping them on the table while they smiled at the irate man.

"We were just pulling your leg man; sorry." Terry said as he tossed the man the money.

The man pulled the rubber band off the roll and his eyes nearly popped out; in his hands was thousands of dollars. He quickly counted out what the cost of the diner was and was about to roll the money back up when Terry stopped him.

SHANE

"Wait bro; pull out a few bonus hundred pound notes and pass them around so everyone get a share for your excellent service tonight; and good humor." Terry said

The waiter did just that he pulled out seven of the notes and handed them out to the staff and then he rolled up the still large roll of cash and tossed it back to Terry with a sheepish grin.

"I am sorry I acted so badly; you gentlemen are the best customers we have ever had. It was a pleasure to spend the evening with you as our guests." The burly waiter said.

Payton looked a little put out on the way back to the private car; both wolves noticed it and they stopped short and Payton noticed their footsteps stopped; and he turned to see why.
Both men were looking at the boy quizzically.

"What?"

"Spill it little brother; something is bothering you and we want to know what that is; because we are your friends." Terry said with a smile.

Payton looked miserable and his eyes dropped to the floor and he seemed like he was not going tot be able to say anything at the current time; so Terry stepped forward and tossed the kid over his shoulder and started walking again.

SHANE

"Okay keep your peace P; when you're ready you can tell me what is on your chest crushing the life out of you." Terry said.

They reached the private car and opened the door to face Ajay's canon pointed at them. Ajay smiled a hard faced smile and lowered the shotgun. Jc gave him his fresh fried chicken and handed a jar and a box to Jazon. Jazon looked at the jar and raised his eyebrows in question.

"Blood."

"Thanks."

"Sure thing; you looked like you were going to chew on us if you didn't get some blood soon Jazon. I thought it would be a nice gesture to bring you a little something. Hey I brought four bottles of ale as well; and they are cold." Jc said.

Jazon and Ajay ate every single bite of the food and drank all four bottles dry. Terry and Payton took the bottle back to the dining car for the hell of it. On their way back; Terry suddenly tensed and snarled. Terry's eyes turn jet black and his muscles bloomed before Payton's rounded eyes. Terry was wolfing out; he grabbed Payton around the waste and grunted "hold on", and then he burst to speed. They were at the private car in one single breath. Terry dropped Payton on his feet and pulled the door open roar in the door. Jc was on his feet and wolfing out in an instant. Jazon was standing up with his sword drawn; Ajay was standing with his gun at the ready.

"Where are they Terry?" Ajay asked.

Terry was all giant werewolf now; so he pointed down the hall and out the window. Jazon did not speak; he just looked at Ajay. The black man shook his head and Jazon nodded.

"Wolves clear the train; and be careful. We will take care of the outside threat; Payton you are with us." Jazon said.

"Hey I can fight; so why not send me with them." Payton said as he pointed at Terry who was on all fours because he was too tall to stand now.

"Simple really kid; they can't talk in wolf form and you can't read there minds, so you could get them killed; I can't allow even the chance of that." Jazon said in a final tone.

If Payton was going to argue; he was not given a chance. Bullets ripped through the window and Payton was standing dead center. The boy realized his life was over in that in that instant; when the first bullets shattered the tempered glass. Something as hard as steel wrapped around Payton suddenly; and he was not hit by the bullets. Payton looked up into the pure crimson eyes of Jazon who was shielding him for the gun fire and Payton was terrified. Jazon was being hit by the bullets and he was not even flinching.

"Are you hit Payton?" Jazon asked.

SHANE

"No." Payton said in a shaky voice. "I did not even see you move; are you fast enough to beat a bullet?"

"Lucky for you P; I was this time." Jazon said with a smile.

Ajay reached out and tossed a suitcase in the window; and then the room was a tornado of action. Jazon tossed Payton in the corner behind Ajay. Ajay pulled a pistol out of the small of his back; held it up; checked the clip; dropped the safety and handed it to Payton.

"Point that at the door; if anyone who is not a wolf comes around the corner put a few of those in them; you have fifteen rounds make them count." Ajay said.

Jazon pull the case out of the window and made a mighty leap through it and was gone. A strange blue eyed vampire popped his head in through the window and Ajay blew his head off his shoulders and grabbed the body before it could fall and blasted a hole through where the heart should be; then he tossed the body off the train. There was a major battle being pitched in the halls of the train. It was so fierce that the train was shaking back and forth. All of a sudden a werewolf that was not Jc or Terry was tossed in front of the suite door, Payton jumped forward stomped on the head as it was trying to rise and put a yellow jacket in the wolf's right eye; and then Payton turned and looked down the hallway to see that his friend was fighting five on one. Payton dropped to one knee; steadied his breath and shot three of the enemy wolves in the head. Terry grabbed the closest living one and snapped its neck and tossed it off the train right through a window. Jc came out of the black hallway and tore the spine out of the last one with his huge clawed hand. Jc looked at Payton with his black eyes and held up his thumb to the kid; as if to say well done. Both wolves came down the hall looking back into the black for any sign of an enemy. Both of them were hurt pretty bad, they were bleeding like a broken dam. Out of the dark came the burly waiter Payton almost shot him; But Terry held up his hand in front of Payton as if to say wait.

"What are you doing here?" Payton yelled down the hallway at the burly man.

The waiter was transfixed at the sight of the werewolves, but his eyes suddenly went to a spot behind Payton. Fast as a pit viper the waiter pulled a huge knife and hurled it down the hall right between Terry and Payton. Payton would have shot the man, but Terry had turned and looked behind them; his huge hand closed softly around Payton's wrist. Payton looked over his shoulder. The wolf Payton shot was sitting up with a knife jutting out of its throat. Terry walked back and grabbed it by the top of its head and in one quick move tossed it out the window Ajay was guarding. Ajay moved as if he was mechanical; right out of the way as the body sailed by, and then stepped back to his post. The burly man was green to the gills, he looked terrified, but he soldiered on.

"I heard the battle and saw your friends turn into..." the waiter tried to say.

SHANE

"They turned into werewolves; because that is what they are." Payton said.

"Yes I see that. They are injured so I brought first aid supplies and a basket of juice and food. I don't know what else to do." The man said.

The entire train was rocked by an explosion and it tossed everyone down to the floor. Ajay was on his feet in an instant peering out the window like a sentinel. He looked worried but only in his eyes. Jc reverted back to fully human and he was tore up pretty bad. Terry stayed all wolfed up and he was sniffing the air. His head turned and he looked at Jc and growled.

"OH shit; it is not over. Kid cover the other end of the hallway; Ajay heads up Terry says there are wolves and vamps on the roof. You the waiter with the good beer get down in the corner and stay low." Jc yelled.

Jc was all wolfed out again standing just between Terry and Payton; looking up at the roof. There was a sudden sharp slam on the roof and a huge back print was clear from the inside. Someone had body slammed a werewolf so hard their body made an imprint in the metal. Ajay leaned out the window and popped off two rounds with his custom shotgun. There were screams of pain and body parts falling passed the window. All the time Ajay's face never change expressions. A few minute later Jazon slipped through the window and collapsed on the floor covered in blood and bullet holes and other rips and tears that would end a person's life. Jazon was lying on the floor gurgling as he breathed; his face was facing the waiter. Suddenly Jazon opened his eyes and even Ajay was scared for the waiter. Jazon's eyes were solid white except for his crimson pupils, his ears were pointed and his fingers had evil looking claws at the end; that dripping blood. Jazon reached out toward the waiter and everyone tensed.

"Howdy; I am Jazon wild. Are you the fine fellow with that wonderful beer I drank before?" Jazon said.

"Erik; I mean that is my name. I am Erik; and yes I am the man with the beer. Are you a vampire?" Erik asked.

"Yes I am; but I would rather have a bottle of your beer than you to drink; I don't do people blood; because I am a people and God says not to eat people." Jazon said shaking Erik's shaking hand.

Jazon rolled over on his back after letting Erik's hand go; he looked terrible. Ajay looked at Jc and the big wolf came to stand by the window. Ajay pulled a caramel sucker out of his pocket and ripped the wrapper off and put it in Jazon's mouth. Ajay looked worried.

"Do you have anymore blood and raw meat Erik?" Payton said.

"Yes; it is in the dining car." Erik said.

"Fine me and my dog will go with you and get it for the boss; he need to rest for now." Payton said looking at Ajay.

SHANE

Ajay nodded to Terry and smiled at Payton. Payton dropped his clip and counted the rounds; and then he popped the clip back in; dropped the safety and led the way. When Erik and the boys were gone Ajay spoke to his friend.

"How close did we come; and how bad off are you?" Ajay asked quietly.

Jazon did not open his eyes; but red tinged tear of pain rolled down his face and onto the floor. Jc was listening but he did not turn his eyes away from the dark night; there were still enemies in that dark and they were not going to get him or any of the other because he was not ready.

"Someone wants us dead pretty bad bro. There were dozens of vamps and wolves on the roof; it was like locust up there. I was not sure I was going to live to make it back here; hell I still might not make it without a lot of blood." Jazon whispered weakly.

There were running foot steps coming down the hallway; Ajay tensed. Jc sniffed the air once and spoke.

"It is Terry and the boy; they are alone." Jc said as he began to wolf down to human again.

Terry was carrying a tub of bloody meat; but that did not draw Ajay's attention; it was the fresh bandage on the boy's right forearm that did. Ajay looked at Payton and the boy held up a finger to his cyanotic lips; and then he held up a jug of red viscous liquid. Ajay did not have to guess at the type of fluid, he knew very well

what it was. Payton was wobbling when he handed over the Jug to Ajay and motioned to Jazon on the floor. Ajay took the jug and took a deep breath and he sat on the floor by Jazon's head; which he lifted up on to his lap. My God Jazon felt all broken to Ajay.
"Hey bro drink this and don't spill any if you want to live." Ajay said sternly.

Jazon put the jug to his lips and drank. Jazon's eyes opened and they were pale red. He jerked the jug away from his mouth and managed not to spill any of it. Ajay grabbed his arm and looked hard at Jazon and then at Payton. Jazon looked at the kid and was instantly ill; Payton looked like a bloodless ghost. Jazon looked at the jug and realized that it would take a lot more than just the boy blood to fill this container.

"Yes; there has been sacrifice; so drink all of it and get strong." Ajay said.

Jazon looked extremely upset; however he tipped the bottle up and drank every single drop of the human blood in the bottle. Jazon was energized in a way he could not believe; and there was a side effect to drinking human blood. Jazon knew the memories of the boy Payton; he saw why Payton hated vampires and it made Jazon so mad he could have started a fire with his eyes.

"It was Mark." Jazon said.

Everyone looked at Jazon like he lost his mind; everyone but Payton; who was looking into Jazon's crimson eyes.

"I know what happened to your family Payton and more; I know who did the deed. I give you my word right here and now; I will not die and let that bastard of a vampire live. His days are numbered kid; the days of Mark O'Day are few and you should know he is our enemy as well as yours." Jazon said.

Ajay looked like he was going to grind his teeth out at the mention of Mark's name. Ajay clearly hated the blood sucker with his entire being; the fire in the black man's eyes said more than Jazon's clear declaration of war. It was at this point that Payton knew he could trust Jazon and his crew; they were solid and loyal; and they had trusted him during a battle; they had not treated him like a child but as a brother.

"Come on kid you need to eat bad." Jazon said.

The vampire swept up the kid and moved so fast that the hallway was a blur. Jazon placed Payton on the chair in the corner; where the table was not broken or dirty. Jazon turned to see that the waiter staff all had bandages on their arms. So this is who gave me back my life.

"I am Jazon Wild; a vampire; but I am not like any vampire you will ever meet. Until this day; I have never tasted human blood. I own my life to you people; thank you." Jazon bowed low and deeply. "My young friend is wiped out and needs food; but I can see that you are all wiped out as well; so I will cook for you."

SHANE

Not one single person argued with Jazon; perhaps they were afraid; but more than likely they were just o tired. Amazingly the dining car was not busted up like most of the rest of the train cars; so Jazon got right to work. He cooked up chicken and homemade dumpling in a huge pot; and then he cooked bread with Erik watching them brown while he was chopping and cooking the salad and the other items. In less than forty minutes Jazon set a good spread out on the huge corner table and Erik helped bring out the dishes and flatware. One of the other waiters helped set out ale and water and some sweat wine. The meal was excellent all of the staff had to admit and Payton had the color returning to his pale face. The staff was surprised when Jazon sat and ate the dumpling and bread with them; he just laughed and explained about himself and his promise to GOD to be strictly speak a white knight. After a short while Ajay and the two wolves came to the dining car because of the excellent aroma. They sat and ate as well.

"What the hell is going on in here; and why are the train cars all ripped apart?" the night conductor bellowed.

Erik jumped up and began to try to explain the story to the weasel faced man; however the guy was not listening until; Erik said vampire. The conductor went into a rage over this.

"That is the most ridiculous story I have ever heard you fat idiot; there is no such thing as vampires or werewolves." The conductor screamed at Erik.

Jazon who was eating a piece of bread just sighed and looked at Terry.

"Show him."

Terry stood up and changed into a full werewolf and looked down into the conductor's pale face. The man peed on himself; Terry reverted to human and sat down and began eating again. Jazon stood up and walked over to the man and spoke to him softly.

"Look at me carefully and don't look away." Jazon said.

Jazon changed; his eye went crimson and his teeth lengthened and sharpened; and his ear was pointed. Jazon grabbed the conductor and ran up the wall and stood with his feet on the roof while still holding the conductor tightly. Jazon flipped and landed lightly on his feet.

"Is that enough of an explanation man or do you need more?" Jazon asked.

"Did you rip up the train?" the conductor asked.

"No; the train was attacked by an army of vamps and werewolves. We four; with the help of the dining staff fought them off and saved the train and our lives. Now, we are having a meal to give thanks for our good fortune; would you like some? Jc said.

"Is that why the train lurched a short while ago?" the man asked.

SHANE

The entire company looked at Jazon; who had a mouthful of hot buttered bread. Jazon swallowed and then cleared his throat.

"That was the chopper blowing up and falling on the caboose. Sorry but as strong as I am; even I can't toss a chopper very far while standing on top of a moving train." Jazon explained.

The silence lasted for a moment and then everyone started laughing nervously at just how close they all came to dying. More; the four; no the five unlikely heroes that gave their all to make sure that only they had to fight the enemy; and not the staff of the train. Amazing; that is what it was; simply amazing.

"Why does this child have a firearm?" the conductor asked.

"When I said the four of us; that was wrong; it was the five of us. Payton shot five of the mongrels down himself; not to mention he is as good with a knife as any man I have ever known." Terry said.

"Terry means that it would be a piss poor idea to try to take the gun from Payton; he might kill you." Ajay said.

"Ok." The conductor said in a meek voice.

The man looked around and everyone knew he was going to ask a question. He did and this time his voice was strong and sure.

SHANE

"Who is going to pay for all of this damage to the train; and all the food that you are all currently eating?" the conductor said.

(laughter)

The conductor did not look pleased at being laughed at; but he was not foolish enough to get bitchy with the monster squad.

"Have they train company go after who ever owned the chopper, that is what damaged the train man. We will pay for all the food mate; so chill out dude." Jc explained.

The conductor actually smiled because it was a great solution to his problem. The conductor thought he was going to have to try to get the funds out of the monsters and he did not see how he was going to be able to do that. The rest of the night went by without any surprises. Ajay paid the bill for the food and the boys went back to their private car and tossed the broken glass out of the window and since it was a strangely warm night they all went to sleep.

(Train whistle)

The train pulled into the Glen Fininen station and it screeched to a halt. The boys were awake and alert at once. They had all their gear in hand and were off the train before it settled to a full stop. Payton was literally being carried like baggage by Terry; because of the incredible speed that the boys were moving. Payton could never even come close to keeping up; therefore

SHANE

Terry very unceremoniously grabbed the boy and then he burst to speed. Payton would have been surprised or angry; but he was way to damn tired. Payton did not have the eternal strength and recuperative powers of the Eternals he was traveling with. It was after the feast that Jazon explained the fact that vampires are not immortal; they are in fact eternals; mean they live a long time without aging. True immortals are rare and secretive about that fact of their existence. Payton had to admit Jazon was a wild guy; the vampire preferred pop to blood and loved fresh baked bread and real butter. Payton did not think that vampires ate food; well not human food anyway; but Jazon did. Jazon was like a regular guy for the most part; that fact messed with Payton's mind. Terry who was a werewolf did not scare Payton at all for some reason; however, Ajay with his dark brooding way and Jc with his deeply aggressive nature that was revenge filled; scare the poop out of him.

A figure at the train station witnessed the leap that Jazon and the boys made from the train and was on a cell phone a seconds later announcing that they were in the Glen and moving toward the castle on the road.

"Hey should we be walking down the road in broad day light or what?" Terry asked.

"That is a good question." Jc added.

Ajay answered in the exact words that Jazon was thinking.

"We are already marked for death; they know we are coming this way; and we know they are going to have another go at us. It is less likely that a bunch of vampires and werewolves are going to attack us in the light of day on a public road." Ajay said and then started walking toward the horizon.

The boys walked for miles and they talked and whistled as they went. They told each other jokes and asked riddles. It was a walking party to all that witnessed it go by. They did not see how combat ready the group looked below the outward mirth. Jc sniffed the air every twelve steps, and he kept Payton between him and Terry at all times; just in case there was bullets flying. Jc liked the kid and did not want to see any harm come to him. Jc felt that Payton and him had a common bond, there life in the last many years was screwed up by vampires.

"Good day to ya lads. Where be you going this fine marning?" asked a grey haired man with a pitch fork.

The werewolves sniffed the man and their eyes narrowed. Jazon could smell it as well and acted to keep the peace; the man was a full human after all and might be forced to act against his will.

"Heel boys; sit, stay. (chuckle)" Jazon said.

Jazon turned and address the man directly.

"Sir we are headed down this road in search of a powerful lord who lives near by. I also see that you have a pitchfork and nothing near by to use it on; therefore I assume that it is only a prop; Your hands are too clean to be a farmer and you smell like a vampire..." Jazon said as his eyes went crimson.

The man smiled and laughed; and then he tossed the pitch fork away and looked at Jazon and the boys speculatively. He seemed to be trying to figure out what he should say or not say. The man knew enough about the group to know they were no to be trifled with.

"Are you alone out here mister?" Jc asked.

"Why yes I am; but why do you ask?" the man said.

Jc looked at Jazon; who shook his head in the affirmative. Jc forged ahead.

"Lately we have experienced a lot of unfriendly behavior from the bulk of the people we meet. We are not the type to let the guilty go free if you follow my meaning. I want to know if we are being set up? Jc explained.

The man was no longer smiling; he felt his life was about to take a turn for the worse. He was told that this group was special and they had been attacked and that the attackers were dead. The man decided to disseminate instead of banter.

"This road will lead you to the home of Sir Collin; he runs the country and owns the land you currently stand on. If you have business in Ireland see him first and save yourself some trouble." The man said.

"I smell fear all over this man; he is too afraid to lie to us; although he did not say it; he is alone out here." Jc said.

The man shuddered in fear as Jc leered at him. Ajay put his hand on Jc's arm and calmed him. He walked over and held out his hand.

"We mean you and no man any harm; we are after two black hearted vampires. I will kill them when I meet them; but you have nothing to fear from us as long as you don't set us up or attacks us personally." Ajay said.

"I would not be so stupid; as to cross slayers such as you; Erik warned me to be up front and Iain spoke with you." The man explained.

"Erik, the policeman?" Ajay asked.

The other boys looked at Ajay; but not Jazon who knew this was a test.

"No Erik is a cook and waiter on the train you just got off; he is also my sister's son. He felt you could use a little guidance; so he sent me to point you where you wanted to go. I have done that I believe and can help you no more. Good bye lads." The older man smiled and turned and walked across the field to a small pick up in the brush and drove back towards the town the boys had just come from.

"Do you think he told us the truth?" Payton said.

SHANE

"Yes, he was scared to death of us. More he knew what we could do to him. Even if he was an enemy; he would know that he could be killed before he could defend himself; yet, he held his ground and spoke plainly with us. He was a brave honest man I think.' Jazon said.

The group did not dally any longer about the chance meeting with the nice man; they set their feet to the road and moved along. Payton who was exhausted but would not say so started to droop as he tried to keep up; so Terry said that he really could use more weigh on his back pack; and he grabbed Payton up and tossed him on the flat top of the pack. Payton did not argue because Terry made it seem that carrying Payton was for Terry's benefit not Payton's; even though the boy knew it was a ploy to save his pride. In truth Terry did enjoy the extra weigh. The group walked for a few hours when they finally came to the hamlet where Sir Collin's home was.

"Hey boys what say we duck into that little shop over there and grab a snack; I am famished." Terry said. "How about you little buddy; hungry?"

"Yah, I could use a drink and a snack; if your all for it mates." Payton said

All four members did not miss the fact that the boy addressed them as mates. He finally accepted them as friends and made the choice to be with them in more than spirit.

SHANE

"Sounds good; besides who knows when we might get another chance to eat before some vermin take another go at us?" Jazon said.

Ajay just grunted and began to walk towards the store or market on the corner. The store owner was a mean faced woman. The woman looked at Ajay and made a evil face; he just looked at the cooler and went to it and snagged at big bottle of Coke and two bottle of Rootbeer. Terry who was not good at finding his feeling gave the owner a sour look and walked over to the isle with the boxes of snack cracker. After only a few minutes all the snacks and drinks were chosen and placed on the counter. Everyone except Ajay left the store; mostly because Jazon shoved them out; they were pissed at the woman's obvious prejudice of Ajay's skin color. Ajay stood there and waited patiently for the woman to ring up the supplies. She just looked at him with hate in her eyes.

"I do not serve your kind." The woman said.

"What kind would that be; American or black?" Ajay asked.

"Get out or I will shoot ya where you stand." The woman shouted as she pulled a pistol.

Ajay smiled and tapped on the counter; the woman looked down to see Ajay's cannon pointed at her belly.

"I don't know why you hate me so much lady; but I have never harmed another person unless they forced me too. Now, how much for all of this stuff; I don't steal either?' Ajay asked.

"One hundred pounds sterling." The woman said with an evil smile as she lowered her gun.

Ajay tossed a hundred pound note on the counter; even though the stuff was worth not much more that forty guinea; and then he smiled and had Terry come collect the stuff as they walked out of the store. Payton was in the doorway looking at the woman.

"You have put the shame on your clan with this dark action; I have always been proud of me heritage; but now I am ashamed to say I am Irish." Payton said glaring at the woman.

The boy turned and walked away without another word. The group walked to the edge of the small town and sat in the shade of a few trees and ate and drank to refresh themselves. After what seemed like an eternity Terry spoke.

"Those were very good word little buddy; you put that old bat in her place. I am frankly surprised she was so speechless." Terry said.

"I evoke her family honor and the stain she just put upon it. We Irish are a proud folk; and we hold our families to be sacred; and our family honor is a greater thing than any one person's honor. So to dishonor your family is a very bad thing." Payton explained.

SHANE

"Yes, I am Irish as well and I understand that; but why did you do it?" Jazon asked.

"I have no family of my own; so I have decided to adopt all of you as my brothers; al least until you go home again; as my brothers; none may question your honor or insult you without a reprisal from myself. I will not allow it; if I did it would stain my honor; which is all I have left." Payton said.

Terry looked heart sick and proud as proud could be as he looked at the boy. Jc looked much the same at that moment. Jc was just as alone as the boy was; he had no clan; he was a loner. Ajay punched Payton in the arm and smiled at him.

"You're not alone anymore little brother; not as long as I am alive; you have my word." Ajay said.

"Okay saddle up kiddies." Jazon said in a funny voice.

The group walked down the road and saw a solver plate on a sign post that pointed down a well groomed paved private drive with a cast iron gate and no talk box or intercom to ask to have the gate opened. In the middle of the gate in had huge fancy plaques with old English writing; they said 'O'Day Castle'.

"So this is where that little bastard Mark ran! Well, it would save him from me." Ajay snarled and pulled his shotgun out.

The angry young black man was about to blow the gate down when Jazon touched his arm and stopped him.

"We want to sneak in man, not have them put the dogs on us; so let me just break the locking mechanism and open the gate quietly bro." Jazon said smiling.

SHANE

CHAPTER 6: BROTHERHOOD

Jazon stepped forward to rip open the lock; but Jc held his arm and looked at the gate intently as if he could see something that should not be there or something that should. Jc let go of Jazon's arm and bent down to pick up a stone; he tossed the stone against the gate and it exploded into dust. Jc just looked at the gate and then he said one word.

"Okay."

Jc wolfed out and was about to ram the gate when Jazon shouted at him to get his attention. Jc stopped and looked at the tiny vampire standing beside him smiling. Jazon tossed a stone over the fence.

"Why don't we just jump the fence and not get all burned up ramming it?" Jazon suggested.

Jc grunted and looked at Terry; Terry was wolfing up; once he was completely transformed he held out a huge paw to Payton. The boy understood and jumped into his friend's arms and then swapped to his mighty back. Terry leaped over the fence by several feet easily. What Terry and the boy did not know was that a silent alarm had been triggered by the stone being tossed over the fence. The manor house was aware they were going to have company. Jc and Jazon who morphed into his faster stronger self; grabbed Ajay under his arms and jumped the fence with no effort. Either Jazon or Jc could have jumped carrying Ajay; however Ajay would

SHANE

not have been able to keep his cannon at the ready if attacked while in the air so they tandem jumped to make sure. Together they walked un-accosted down the well maintained drive. Terry grunted something and Jc growled back. Jc stopped and pointed at points on both sides of the drive; there were cameras and they were on and recording. Jazon, who was being a card; walked over to one of the cameras and waved at it.

"Hello there in the house; we are coming to visit; sadly the gate was closed and unattended so we were forced to let ourselves in." Jazon said.

Terry and Jc were very tense and they next wolfed back down; instead they seemed to become more feral not less. Ajay looked at them and reached over and pulled Payton back a a few steps.

"Nothing personal P; but I think the dogs are on a mission right now and they will strike without thinking; so give them a little more ground." Ajay said.

Terry turned his black glowing eyes to Ajay's and nodded once and then burst into the trees along the side of the drive and was gone. Jc did the same on the opposite side of the road; he silently blended with the night. Now for those of you who don't know a full werewolf is about the only thing that can stand up against a vampire. However, this manor house and the keep around it contains a master vampire; perhaps the most powerful on the planet.

"Be ready little brother; but try to hold back on the trigger finger unless you have no choice; after-all we are so trespassing here." Jazon chuckled.

"I'm solid bro; so is Payton." Ajay said.

Payton wondered how the black man knew he had the Glock in his left hand and a knife in the other hand; neither showed. Later, Payton scolded himself; he needed to pay attention to his surroundings. There was nothing to be worried about as it turned out. The owner of the manor wanted to meet them and he sent no guards to fetch them to him. Collin was a very patient man; to rush a volatile first meeting like this one was to be; could very well end badly for everyone. Collin was not arrogant enough to believe he could not be harmed or that his staff and person belongings could not destroyed if they got in the way of an angry adversary.

"Okay Payton were are about to go into the manor house and it could be a death trap and I don't want you to be dead so be very careful not to take any chances; because I won't be leaving anything to chance." Jazon said.

Payton looked at Jazon but he was looking at Ajay; the face they showed each other was about trust and brotherhood and caution; although neither would likely step away from any challenge. Payton was not insulted at Jazon's warning; because it was meant as a friend out of caring and not patronizing like most adults extend towards kids.

SHANE

"One more thing little buddy; don't stand to close to me; I seem to get shot at a lot and I don't want you to get caught up in that." Ajay said with a twisted evil smile that promised pain to come.

(Laughter)

Jazon and Ajay broke out in deep real laughter; it seemed misplaced to Payton but then again he had not been in as many wars as these guys had and all together. They must have some inner personal joke that they are currently enjoying.

"Ready?" Jazon asked.

"Always bro." Ajay said.

Jazon motioned for the wolf bay to run ahead and scout while the three of them walked into the keep and continued to the manor proper. The wolves moved like well oiled killers; which of-course they were. All werewolves were trained in the arts of combat and death from the first time they turned; it was for their own protection. Terry and Jc were elite even among other werewolves; only wolf and perhaps Enoch could beat Terry in an open brawl. Jc was an unknown quantity, but he was a bad ass and merciless in combat and he was big; his head was five inches higher than Terry's when the stood all the way up as wolves. Jc was special as well; he could do something that is very rare; he could take the form of an actual wolf and run faster than wolf could think of and he was silent as death.

SHANE

The manor house was old and new at the same time. It was gorgeously built and regal in every way. The front door was made of solid hard wood and it had the house crest on it. Jc was going to kick the door in but Ajay stopped him by clearing his throat. Ajay stepped up and rang the door bell. The manor house was alive with a jingling music that was pleasant and serviceable at the same time. All five of the boys tensed as the door began to open; they were combat ready.

"Yes can I help you?" an older gentleman asked.

The man was dressed in green and was older but stout and well muscled from toil. His hands were strong and scarred from working a hard labor job. However, the man smelled like a vampire; only the scent was different and tossed the boys for a loop.

"You know damn well we are expected mister; stop wasting our time and invite us in." Payton said.

The older man made a sour face at the boy and was about to strike him across the face' when Terry's huge hand grabbed the old man and lifted him off his feet.

"Take it easy gramps." Terry growled in a gravel-like voice.

To the older man's credit he seemed unimpressed by Terry's werewolf body; and the fact he was being held by a ten foot werewolf in general. Terry was pretty sure this man had seen his kind before; because his heart never sped up when he was grabbed. Terry placed the man on his feet and snarled at him.

SHANE

"**Behave yourself old man.**" **Terry scolded him.**

(Gentle laughter came form the doorway)

All eyes were on a new arrival. He was a good looking man in his late twenties and had the clearest blue eye any of them had ever seen. The man smiled and his fangs showed; a vampire then; no missing that.

"**Please come in and be welcome in my home.**" **The vampire said.**

The group followed the new vampire into the manor. The host led them to a grand meeting hall with many chairs and end tables between them. He stopped and looked at the werewolves.

"**You will not be attacked in my home; you have nothing to fear here.**" **The vampire said.**

"**Bullshit blood sucker; the fact you are a vampire means only lies comes out your mouth.**" **Jc growled in perfect English despite being totally wolfed out. That was something else that was unusual about him.**

"**Am I addressing Sir Collin?**" **Jazon asked.**

Before he could answer another person walked into the hall; and that was when all hell broke loose.

"**MARK!**" **Ajay screamed.**

SHANE

The fast black man pulled his cannon and blasted the door way behind Mark so that the vampire had to stop or die. Mark turned and glared at Ajay with fear in his eyes.

"How dare you..." Collin snarled.

The lord of the manor tried to pull his deadly sword; however in that instant he was slammed into the wall with Jazon's dagger across his throat.

"Private matter; stay out of it or you can be killed as well." Jazon said.

Collin looked into Jazon's white eyes with red pupils and then looked at his own hand that was still holding the hilt of his sword. Over the top of his own hand was Jazon's; it was impossible to pull his sword. Collin tried to exert his strength over the young vampire and found that he could not even budge his hand. So he changed tactics.

"Yes, I am Sir Collin O'Day."

"Nice that explains a lot in a short period of time." Jazon said.

"Who are you and why do you want my great grandson?" Collin asked.

Mark tried to bolt for a window but he met Jc face to face; and Terry had blocked the rear entrance. Mark was trapped. Ajay walked forward and looked Mark in the face.

SHANE

"I want the cure for Silky boot licker or your dead; and I mean final death; a painful, miserable death." Ajay said calmly.

"Your preety brave with you hunter allies; but yer a coward without them to help ya." Mark said.

Ajay lifted both eyebrows and then he turned and walked over to Jazon.

"Lend me you twins Brother; I don't want there to be any mistake here and now." Ajay said.

Jazon did not speak of turn his gaze away from Collin; he just shook his head. Ajay reach under the back of Jazon's leather jacket and pull two blue hilted sword swords. Ajay walked across the room and placed his 12 gauge autoloader cannon on the end table in front of Jc and then slide off his other weapons and his leather duster. Ajay took the sword out of the scabbards and walked over to Mark.

"Is he just going to kill Mark like an animal while we watch?" Collin asked in a civilized tone.

"Just watch my boy work Collin and learn the truth." Jazon said as he loosened the blade from Collin's throat.

The lord of the manor watched in curiosity as the black human male approached Mark with two blades in his powerful hands. Ajay stopped and addressed Mark and the room.

"This is a personal matter Mark; you have poisoned my woman and I am going to kill you for it; or you can give me the antidote and save her. If you choose to help I will let you live, if not we fight until one of us wins or is dead. There will be NO interference from anyone; we fight one on one alone; winner takes all." Ajay explained.

"Fine, I choose to fight you then human. You are going to die just like your bitch..."Mark started to say.

Ajay hit Mark so hard with an uppercut that the vampire back flipped. Ajay tossed the sword on the floor by Marks hand; and then he took a combat pose. Mark sprang to his feet and tried a frontal attack; this was a mistake because Ajay was ready for that. Jay just side stepped the blade as Mark thrust it at him and cut off Marks left ear and some scalp. Mark howled in pain and turned and tried to gut Ajay in a fast sweeping move across the black man's body. Mark got a huge surprise, the blade raked across something and it did not enter Ajay's body. Ajay kicked Mark in the balls sending him tears in eyes to his knees.

"Damn boy that looked painful; can you still pee out that broke faucet?" Jc asked as he laughed without humor.

Collin's eyes narrowed at Jc in anger; Jc looked at him with the unmistakable; anytime you want to try me look on his wolfed up mug. Ajay ignored everyone he addressed Mark only.

SHANE

"Will you pleased just help me save Silky; it is really Brian we want not you mate. I will kill you if you don't help me though." Ajay said sternly.

Mark did not answer; rather he sprang up and tackled Ajay to the ground. Mark pinned Ajay's sword hand down and was about to bite Ajay's throat; when Ajay broke Mark's nose with his forehead. Mark jerked his head back and managed to rake Ajay's face with his finger nails; leaving three perfect bleeding stripes. Ajay grabbed Mark's neck and tossed him off to the side. Ajay was on his feet looking at Mark; who had lost his sword over in the corner where Terry stood growling. Mark looked at Ajay and the sword in his hand. Ajay tossed the sword over on the floor by Jc's feet.

"Fine with me; hand to hand works." Ajay said; answering the look Mark gave him.

Mark's nails grew long and sharp and his teeth became longer and pointed. Mark advanced on Ajay who did not move away or circle. Mark launched himself at Ajay. Just as mark was about to rake Ajay's face off; the black pro football player dropped and soccer kicked Mark in his already sore nuts. Mark went down for a second time in a pile of pain and misery; this time Ajay was not going to chat with him. The human got up and walked over and stomped on Mark's foot shattering the bones in his foot. Mark wailed and grabbed for his foot; Ajay stepped on his hand with his right foot and brought the left Nike hi-top down on Mark's hyper-extended elbow shattering it. Ajay was far from finished; but he paused.

"I am going to stop asking soon and just finish you off; will you tell me how to save my girl?" Ajay asked.

"YES, stop hurting me." Mark screamed.

Ajay grabbed Mark up off the floor and tossed him is a chair like a sack of grain. Meanwhile, Connor saw Jazon holding a blade to Collin's throat; He pulled two knives and hurled them expertly at vulnerable spots on a vampires back and neck. Out of nowhere two flat silver blades knocked Connor's right out of the air. Connor's head jerk around and he was about to toss a new volley of blades at the hidden attacker. He stopped as the tiny human stepped out of the curtains with ten blades protruding between in fingers of both his hands. The boys faced each other like enemies. Payton and Connor did not know each other; because they thought the other was dead. Payton was faster handed when it came to throwing blades; Payton sent ten pure silver blades buzzing toward Connor in a blur of movement. Connor tossed his larger blades after a fast sideways motion; therefore he stopped four out of ten blades coming at him. Connor did however take two serious slashes across his body. Payton was already moving and spinning blades into the air; trying for everything he was worth to kill his opponent. One of the blades was ricocheted over his dagger and it nearly hit Collin. It went right between Collin and Jazon's faces and sank into the wall. They both jerked their heads back; when they did Jazon removed his hand and Collin pulled his sword.

"Ha!" Mark exclaimed as he dove on Ajay and pulled a knife from his pocket.

SHANE

Mark jumped on Ajay and stabbed him in the color bone where the armored undershirt did not protect him. Ajay did not scream or even flinch; he just hit Mark in the jaw with a hard right hook. Mark's jaw broke and he fell over stunned.

Collin went stab Jazon with his sword and Jazon blocked the assault with Soul Stealer his magical long sword. Collin was surprised; he continued to attack until Collin laughed at him.

"You are clumsy with your sword boy." Collin said.

In a movement so fast Collin could not even see it; Jazon grabbed his blade out of his hand and slammed Collin into the marble wall behind him. Before Collin could react Jazon had both swords across Collin's neck in a scissor move.

"It was a ploy and I fell for it." Collin said; it was not a question.

"Yes, I was playing to your vanity. Your skills are fantastic to behold but painfully slow to me." Jazon said.

Just then a knife hit the wall slicing through Jazon's neck as it went by.

"Damn it Payton; take that guy out or I will." Jazon snarled.

SHANE

"Stop Connor; do not fight anymore. I have lost my contest and you are gravely injured; you will not win if you keep going." Collin said.

"PAYTON?"

"CONNOR!"

The boys looked at each other for a moment and then they both had tears on their young cheeks. The boys ran toward each other; however Amus misunderstood and thought they were still fighting and pulled a gun to shoot Payton.
(BAM)

In a force of moment that actually hurt Jazon; he grabbed Payton just as the bullet was touching his body and pulled the boy out of the way. Collin's eyes were wide with wild wonder at the amazing feet of action. Jazon had blood in his mouth when he stopped right beside Jc. Collin looked at Jazon with the eyes of a scholar; he was intrigued completely now. Twice the vampire had him at his mercy and both times he chose to not kill him...why?

"Oh shit Payton; are you okay? Did that stupid old fart shoot you?" Connor was running to his brother.

Payton was still dazed by the force of the acceleration and subsequent stoppage. Payton saw his brother stop right in front of him; and then he was dangling in Connor's powerful arms; having the life crushed out of him.

"I am okay brother. I thought you were dead." Payton managed to say.

Collin crossed the room between Ajay and Mark with his sword once more in his hand. Ajay tensed for battle; and so did the wolves. Collin however, addressed Mark.

"What do you know about this man's woman; and do you know the antidote for the poison used against her?" Collin asked in a stern voice.

Mark visibly trembled at the gaze of Collin.

"No sir; only Brian knows that and he is missing; I can't say where he is." Mark said.

Collin turned and addressed Ajay.

"Does that ring true to you Moore?" Collin asked.

"It sadly sounds like the truth from this idiot." Ajay said as he put pressure on the stab wound.

"Very well. Mark you might be my blood; but you have disgraced our family long enough; and you have brought hunters to my home. Good bye Mark O'Day last of my relatives." Collin said.

In a swift precise move Collin beheaded Mark and split his heart in two places. Collin sheathed his blade and turned to Ajay. He bowed deeply.

"Amus burn this trash for me. Young man; my family is exceedingly ashamed of that one." Collin pointed at the floor where Amus was gathering body parts to burn. "Come you are in need of medical attention; we are no longer adversaries; therefore please accept my hospitality."

The werewolves walked up very close to Payton and Connor and sniffed them both; at once they both reverted to human form.

"It would seem that our new little brother has found his brother strangely enough." Jc said.

"Yep, they both smell the same; there is no doubt that big kid is P's bro." Terry added.

Jazon was watching Amus clean up the parts when he suddenly bolted forward and began to frisk the dead vampire's body. Everyone looked at him as if he had come loose of his senses; until he produced a cell phone and Mark's wallet.

"Aha, I knew that little bastard was lying his arse off." Jazon said.

"What do you mean bro?" Ajay said.

Ajay wobbled and went to one knee; Jazon started to move; however Collin had already scooped the black man up and was moving as a incredible speed toward the far hallway. Jazon and the boys followed him. Collin kicked a door open and walked in; Jazon went in behind him and found that the room was a ER; complete with all the amenities. Ajay was laid on the table and Collin pulled a sterile scalpel off the surgery tray and began to cut away Ajay's black cotton blood soaked tee shirt. Collin stopped and chuckled.

"Well what is this; I see you have a fine armorer in your house by the Mithril silver shirt your shadow currently wears vampire slayer. Come here and help me ease it off of this boy before he bleeds to death." Collin ordered Jazon.

Jazon Looked at the lord of the manor and he hesitated; on one hand his friend was gravely injured; on the other hand if he got in close to this vampire and helped take off Ajay's only protection; and it turned into a death match, Ajay could die. Collin saw that scenario roll through Jazon's soft crimson eyes and he laughed.

"I give you my word of honor as the ruler of Europe, I will not attack you or your party in any way and neither will anyone in my employ. Does that satisfy you?" Collin asked.

"Yes and I will hold you to your words." Jazon said.

Together Jazon and Collin slipped off Ajay's Mithril shirt which is no easy task; Ajay is a manly man; meaning he is no light weigh. Collin numbed the injury with Marcaine and began to explore the extent of the injury. Collin used some fine nosed clamps to remove two little bone chips; and then he had Jazon hold Ajay down while he set the collar bone back where is should be. Ajay nearly flung both vampires across the room. So, to say that it hurt is a weak statement. Collin expertly sutured up the wound inside and outside of Ajay's body.

"Well, I guess that is all that can be done except giving him a shot for pain and oral medication to keep the pain and infection in check." Collin said.

"Thanks; but no; that is not all that can be done." Jazon said.

Jazon took a sterile scalpel and cut his wrist; he grabbed Ajay's chin and opened his mouth and let his blood drip in his friend's mouth. Ajay opened his eyes and they were red tinged; he looked at Jazon hard; but he swallowed the blood. Collin was amazed; Ajay's severe injury was healing as he watched. Jazon took his arm away and licked the wound and it healed up almost instantly.

"That is a rare ability young hunter." Collin said.

"What is and why don you keep calling me hunter?" Jazon asked.

Collin smiled at Jazon and then patted Ajay on the arm. He walked to the door and gestured for them to follow him. Ajay grabbed Jazon's arm and used it to steady himself enough to sit up and get off the table. Ajay grabbed his Mithril shirt and walked to the sink and washed the blood out of it; then he slung it over his massive shoulders and walked out the door with Jazon on his heels. Collin was waiting at the end of the hallway; the boys joined him. Together they walked down the halls and up a short flight of stairs to a sitting room with a lovely view of the country side. Collin excused himself and a very cute girl of no more than fifteen came in with a tray that had tea and cookies.

SHANE

The girl was staring unashamed at Jazon. She smiled and just stood there.

"Hello girl; what is on your mind?" Jazon asked.

The girl put down the tray on the table and stepped back and addressed both Ajay and Jazon.

"I want to ask you to clarify a few things for me and the house staff if you please." The girl said sweetly.

"Okay shoot darling; what do you want to know." Jazon said.

"I want to know if it is true your shadow is a pure human; and that he beat the master's vampire kin by himself? I also want to know if it is true that you beat the master with a blade and that you can move so fast you can beat a bullet already fired?" the girl asked.

"Yes."

The girl looked confused at Jazon's single word answer. Ajay poured some tea for both Jazon and himself. Then he handed a cookie to Jazon and sat back and sipped his tea out of the expensive cups Collin used. Ajay looked at the completely agog girl and smiled.

"My little brother means yes to all of your questions; I am human and I beat the poop out of Mark alone. Jazon is so fast that he has been known to avoid bullets and he took Collin without having to kill him. Does that satisfy you sugar?" Ajay said pushing the cookie in his mouth.

Collin walked in and smiled. He was dressed in clean clothing and he smelled like fresh flowers. He also heard the girl and addressed her.

"My odd new guests are among the greatest warriors I have ever known, they appear to be capable of amazing feats of physical performance; I am in awe of them. I might add that this gentleman spared my life not once but twice; when he had me at his mercy. Now run along Kelli; I wish to talk with them alone." Collin said.

(Meanwhile down stairs)

The brothers could not be parted; if anyone who had known them in the nearly two years since the death of their family; saw the emotions they were showing they would never have believed it. Both brothers had been cold blooded killers and their prey were mostly vampires; who are at the top of the bloody food chain baby. If you said these boys had grit, you would be understating their iron will and steel spine; not to mention brass do-dads. Terry was sitting on the counter in the kitchen when Kelli walked in and brushed up against him.

"Get off the counter you mongrel." Kelli ordered.

Terry is a nice person if you're his friend; however he is a ruthless mother; if you are not. Terry slid off the counter and popped Kelli on the butt. She turned and slapped his face. Terry did not move or flinch; what he

SHANE

did do was smile and pick the girl up in his arms and kissed her softly on her ruby lips. For all Terry's combat ability and the death around him; Terry was only fifteen and Kelli was beautiful. Kelli tried to squirm away but she was held gently but firmly to Terry. Kelli stopped struggling and kissed him back nicely. Terry's heart was pounding and so was Kelli's when he set her in her feet and stood up to his full height of 6'3. Kelli just looked at him and then took his hand in hers.

"I am sorry I said unkind words to you boy; your embrace was sweet indeed. I have never felt a kiss so sweet before; and because I am choosy
I have had very few kisses. How long are you staying here love; I would like to spend a wee bit more time in your powerful arms." Kelli said with rosy cheeks.

"I am staying until I leave; that is the only answer I can give. I am a soldier after a fashion and my leader gave me a command to protect Jazon and Ajay; I can not go back on my word. I do however want to spend all the time with you I can. You stir my blood Irish girl; like no other ever has and I have never kissed a girl before you. I will measure every kiss from here on out by the sweet taste of your lips on mine." Terry explained.

"Well said kiddo." Jc said "Why don't you and lil miss muffet go play house; I can watch the farm for now. You two are young and excited about life; you should share that while you have it."

Jc looked miserable as he spoke; there was some inner pain that he was carrying with him. Terry would not have left his friend like this if his heart was not screaming at him to be with Kelli.

"Thanks man; I owe you one." Terry said.

Terry scooped up Kelli and burst out the door as if Jc might change his mind. Kelli did not know Terry was a werewolf, but she was about to find out the hard way. Terry ran out into the keep; Kelli pointed to the steps that went up to the side of the castle wall. There was a small guard shack there; it was not used by anyone very often. The shack had coffee, tea and some small supplies in it; it also had blankets for when Collin set off fireworks at night and it got cold; that way the human staff could stay warm and still enjoy the show. Kelli pushed the door open and Terry still holding her in his arms ducked through the door and closed it with his elbow.

"Let's roll out a blanket and cuddle Yankee boy." Kelli said and then she giggled.

Terry was a soldier and was used to doing everything for himself; so when Kelli started to cater to him and make a snack for him; it made him uncomfortable and she noticed.

"What is the matter boy?" Kelli said in a sweet Irish accent.

"Terry."

"Hmmm?"

SHANE

"Kelli, my name is Terry; and I am used to doing everything for myself; so I feel a tad useless now that you are doing everything and I am just sitting her on the floor." Terry told Kelli.

Kelli smiled and Terry's heart melted. She came over and crawled into his laps and his arms. Kelli kissed him on the lips softly and whispered in his ear.

"Just so ya know; I have never let a boy kiss me before you did. I am kind of a hard case you know; so boy leave me be." Kelli whispered in Terry's ear.

"It would not stop me; you are simple divine Kelli; in everyway. You make my heart flop in my chest just being near you." Terry said.

"Oh if you knew any hot girls; you would not find me desirable." Kelli said.

(Laughter)

"Sweetie, you should see Jax, Pegi and Silky; they are full grown young women back home and they are so hot the men around them have their heads swimming all the time. Silky is the reason we are here; she was poisoned by that no good Mark and Brain; Silky is Ajay's woman. Jax is Jazon's girl and Pegi is a crazy elf witch; but we all love her; she is over 200 years old and looks twenty and smoking hot. She is half naked all the time and so are the elves and faeries, but I never felt like I do when I am near you. My breath catches in my chest and I get high." Terry said slowly.

SHANE

Kelli blushed and decided they had talked enough. She leaned into Terry and pressed her lips firmly to his. It was like the night exploded between them; it was more than puppy love; and completely different than lust. It was pure fire; they both felt it at once; they were a match set; the warrior and the princess; the beauty and the beast. They stayed locked in the gentle loving embrace as the night wore on.

In the sitting room Collin was talking like an old friend with Jazon and Ajay. They drank a lot of very good Japanese green tea; it is the best you know. Collin wanted to know more about the boys. They told him the entire story; Jazon started with the fact it was Mark who made him. Collin was startled.

"What is the matter Sir Collin?" Ajay asked.

"When a vampire's sire is killed they usually get very ill or die instantly; you however did neither Jazon. Please just call me Collin."

Ajay began where Jazon left off and two boys explained as much as they could up to the train; and then each of them looked hard at Collin. The master vampire knew when danger was a foot; this was that moment.

"Just say your piece boys; we must be able to speak freely if we are to be friends." Collin said.

"We have been attacked every step of the way since we arrived in London; and we have a near tragedy as a merc force took apart the train we were on. We killed or

SHANE

maimed all of the attackers and kept the train staff out of it by some God given miracle, but they are going come after us again I am sure. Do you have anything to do with that black business Collin?" Jazon asked.

Jazon and Ajay studies Collin's handsome face for any sign of malice or guile. There simply was none.

"I am called Sir Collin; I am a night and the lord high protector of all of Europe. I am the law here; I do not need low life trash to do my bidding, if I wanted to kill you I would do it myself. (Chuckle) Well, I would have tried in your case Jazon." Collin said.

"Hey vampires; I am just a little boy kid from the Couve; I get tired and need sleep unlike you all; so please forgive me if I drift off to sleep." Ajay said as he leaned his head back to rest.

Jazon looked the window and was shocked to see the sun would be up in an hour or so. All of this mess chewed the entire night up; small wonder his mortally wounded brother was spent. Collin saw Jazon's expression and misunderstood.

"Don't worry that is lead glass; it does not let through the sun; you wont' be harm if we stay here as the sun comes up." Collin said.
"Huh...oh, don't worry I am immune to the sun man, and everything thing else vampires are allergic too." Jazon said.

(KA-BOOM)

The entire manor shook violently. Jazon and Collin were on their feet glued to the window; when Ajay jumped out of his chair. Collin jumped across the room and hit what looked like a thermostat. A klaxon went off immediately. Collin was speaking to the picture on the wall; both boys just looked at him oddly like he had lost his mind. However, they both heard the last word he said clearly ...Siege.

"Jc...GUN!" Ajay screamed.

Out of nowhere the giant werewolf appeared and tossed Ajay his cannon and his leather duster. Jc looked behind him and Payton ran in and handed Jazon his short swords and Soul Stealer his might mystical long sword. Connor was standing behind his brother with an Uzi and five clips; a bandolier full of knives and a lot of attitude. Payton smiled and opened his jacket to show the Glock with extra clips and a second pistol with a silencer on the barrel; not to mention a shit-load of his flat deadly blades.

"Just say the word boss and we are on it." Payton said.

Jazon looked at Connor and the older boy winked and put his hand on his brother's shoulder. The meaning was clear, I am with him.

"Jc find Terry and scout; we are no doubt the reason that the manor is being attacked. Brothers find your way out into the keep and make sure the human population is not being cut down; protect them; get them to safety. I know you boys...I mean young men are tough as nails; but live for the next contest; be careful

SHANE

P; I am just getting used to your fresh mouth way."
Jazon chuckled.

"I do my best boss. Hey you the old vampire lord; where
should we send the people if there is shooting so they
can live?" Payton asked.

"Take Amus when you go, he is tough and knows the
keep; tell him I said to support you two and he will."
Collin said.

There was a second explosion and part of the outer
wall fell in. Collin's face was a mask of death. Who ever
was out there picked the wrong Vampire F with. Collin
still had his sword, but he walked over to the mini
couch and slapped the back of it. The entire couch
flipped over. The bottom of the couch had high powered
assault rifles secured to it. Collin took two P90 rifles off
and handed one to Jazon; then gave his a few clips.

"I know you don't trust me son; but my home is being
attacked right now; so I need you to trust me and help
me save my families and our homes from the trash that
would destroy it." Collin practically begged.

Jazon and Ajay looked at each other and then spoke
in one voice.

"We are with you Collin."

The three men ran down the stair toward the ER
room when Terry in wolf form came ripping down the
hall from the other side; snarling out of his mind. Collin
nearly shot him. Ajay grabbed his arm and ran passed

him to Terry. It was when he got close enough he saw that the monster sized Terry had a bloody injured girl in his massive arms; and the wolf wail not snarling he was crying his heart out.

"Oh shit; in here now Terry." Ajay yelled.

Collin ran into the ER and stopped dead; and in a flash had Terry on his back with a knife to his throat. Terry did not even fight back. Jazon was about to drill Collin when a weak voice stopped everything as if it were in slow motion.

"Leave my Terry alone Collin; not his fault. I love him." Kelli whispered.

Kelli was so broken looking and bleeding to death. Collin jumped off Terry and he gave him a hand up; and then he went to Kelli and looked at her like she was his own little injured daughter; Collin's eyes filled with tears of blood. He turned and grabbed Terry by the arm and led him out into the hall. Jazon was afraid for the boy.

"Become a man for me son; I can't talk with an animal." Collin said in a sad voice.

Terry became his human self and tear flew from his eyes the entire time; and there was a deeper volcanic anger within his eyes. Collin put his hand on the boys shoulder and got to the point without hesitation.

"Kelli is human and she is dieing son; the only way to save her is for either you or me to bite her; that means turning her." Collin said firmly.

"Then we better asked her while she can answer; because I won't live without her." Terry said.

The boy turned and walked in he stood up tall and he touched Kelli so gentle with his massive hands. He got down on his knees beside the bed and looked deeply into the dieing girls eyes.

"I love you little girl; now listen to me baby. You have been killed by the scum that attacked this place; don't worry I will kill all of them before I rest; but that aside; I will not let you die. You can be saved if Collin turns you into a vampire or I can...I can make you like me Kelli or you can choose to die; but if you do I will meet you in death after I am done killing that bastards that did you in." Terry spoke well, and he was unable to keep from crying.

"You do it Terry; you're my life; my soul mate; I can't leave you alone here and I can't be your opposite either. (Kelli looked at Collin) I love you like a father Collin; you know that; and I have always wanted to live as long as I could with you because I love you; but I found my one true love be beautiful mistake and now I can't be parted from him ever." Kelli said as blood trickled out of her mouth and she coughed.

"Do it now boy before you loose her." Collin yelled.

SHANE

Totally ignoring Collin; Terry spoke softly and directly to Kelli.

"There will be pain baby; endure it and you will know a strength you can only dream of afterwards." Terry said and then he bit her shoulder hard.

Terry cried as he buried his teeth into his love; it hurt him to have to hurt her. She had a ghostly white face when he bit her; suddenly her blue-green eyes went black and she screamed so load the glass beaker near her on the shelf shattered; and then she smiled and closed her eyes. Collin nearly killed Terry in that instant. Jazon grabbed him and held him in his iron embrace and said a single word to Collin.

"Listen."

Collin did listen and he heard the most welcome sound ever; he heard Kelli's heart beating fast and strong. Jazon let the lord go and started toward the door. Kelli opened her eyes and looked directly into Terry's.

"Go kill them all before they hurt anyone else." Kelli said in a feral tone.

"You don't have to ask twice. Collin please stay with her; she is still so weak and helpless; and I don't want anyone sneaking in here to hurt her or to be hurt by her. So is going through the wild time; and since I can't be here because I have a job that must be done; I need a strong person who she can't kill by accident to watch

SHANE

over her." Terry said as his eyes went black as crude oil.

"We will save your home Collin and people as well; they should not have come here and the sun is now up so...they can't hide this time." Ajay said in a flat tone.

'So be it gentlemen." Collin said.

Amus and the brothers ran into some mercs; the boy told Amus to save the staff; they would put out the trash. Amus almost laughed until he witnessed the brothers fighting without restraint. My God Amus thought as the twisted sidewinders went into a tornado of flying death; never had Amus ever witnessed anyone that good with blades; but then again these young men hunted vampires separate and alone for two years; they were tough and fearless. The mercs were cut to dog food in moments; the boys pulled their blades out of the dead and wiped them off and continued to patrol the grounds as they were bid to do. When he was able Amus followed along behind them and sent the human staff to safety. The brothers never spoke and relaxed, Amus did not speak either for safety sake.

Ajay was sore and hurting not that he would ever say it, but even with Jazon's amazing speed Terry was a blur of fur. Jazon stopped by the outer wall. Collin's staff knew that they were on the same side and so were Jc and Terry. Terry saw; what looked like an army company coming toward the breach in the main wall; Terry arched his back and transformed all the way. Sheesh, he was bigger and meaner looking than Jazon or Ajay ever saw him before; Enoch's word came to Jazon's mind suddenly. "Terry is special and he is a

SHANE

warrior of a different breed, one day he will lead the pack and stand unchallenged for a thousand years".

Terry went after the mercs like they were wheat to his reaper; only he was the reaper and their lives were the wheat. Ajay was going to shoot a few soldier- mercs but he saw Jazon sniffing the air. Without looking at Ajay he said.

"They are all human; so don't waste your special ammo on those trash. Besides, I don't think I would get in Terry's way right now; no matter the odds. They hurt his girl; that will make all the difference. I believe he intends on killing them all himself; but if any try to run drop them." Jazon said.

Jazon was talking only to Ajay but Collin's person mini army answered.

"Yes Sir."

Collin had an extremely loyal group of human commandos; they set up along the wall turrets and shot anyone who got to close to the keep, minus the two juggernauts in wolf's clothing. Terry was a truly monstrous killing machine; he ripped the mercs into piece so fast that the air looked like it was raining blood or a red fog was setting in.

"Shit, remind me to never set that boy's temper off for any reason." Ajay said.

"He is keeping his word to Kelli; all of those fools should run and hope Collin's guards don't shoot them

SHANE

down. I would rather be shot than have Terry get a hold of me if I were them." Jazon said.

A bullet hit Jazon dead center mass and launched him backwards. Ajay looked out at the field and was pulled behind the wall just as a 50cal bullet tore a chunk out of the wall. Connor looked at Ajay.

"You good man?" Connor asked.

"Yeah, thanks I'm good." Ajay answered.

Jazon sat up and looked out over the battlefield and suddenly his eyes locked on a single spot. Jazon was behind the wall and he shouted.

"Everyone down; sniper in the trees." Jazon hollered.

Jazon gave his weapons to Jazon and Connor. He held out a hand to Connor; Connor went to shake it; but Jazon reached passed his hand and drew a knife off his belt. Jazon held it up and smiled; although his blood crimson eyes said he was not joking around. Jazon stepped out and screamed stop. The entire battle field stopped and looked his way. He walked slowly through the battle field, the mercs saw his eyes and knew to leave this man alone. The sun was fully up and the leader of the mercs stepped in front of Jazon.

"Suns up blood sucker, too late to find cover now." The cocky fools said.

Ajay thought Jazon would kill him but he did not. He just pushed him out of the way and kept walking. The leader turned and pointed his rifle at Jazon's back and he laughed.

"Jc would you kill that fool for me?" Jazon whispered; which means everyone heard it clear as a crystal bell.

The leader turned to see a ten foot nightmare drooling blood down his mighty chest.

"Bye bye." Jc said in a gruff tone.

In one quick movement Jc tore the man in two pieces. The sniper in the brush shot Jc in the chest; like that did anything but make him mad. Then the sniper not understanding how dead he already was shot Jazon in the gut. Jazon smiled as his own blood oozed out his guts and mouth; and then he burst to speed; completely disappearing. The sniper heard a branch snap and rolled over to look up at Jazon.

"How?"

"Vampire."
"But sunshine?"

"Immune."

"Shit."

"Yah."

Jazon cut the snipers head off and burst to speed; he stopped in the middle of the field covered in blood. Jazon held up the snipers head and yelled, "Enough!"

SHANE

All movement stopped again.

"I will give each of you the same fate as this guy if you don't tell me who sent you here?" Jazon said.

A fat bald guy stepped forward and addressed the angry vampire.

"I was a homeless lad in London when a vampire who said his names was Brian Finney pay me to come here and shot... well you." The man said.

"Did any of you actually get paid before you came here?" Jazon asked.

The entire merc force looked around at the mercs left alive and they knew they had been cheated. The mini war stopped right there and then; the problem was; Terry was still insane with anger and was out for blood. It is also worth mentioning Terry was riddled with bullet holes and was bleeding like a colander full of hot water. Jc also saw the problem and went to Terry and growled something in his ear. Terry looked sullen; but did not move. Ajay understood the look and acted accordingly.

"Leave now and never hunt us again. If we ever see any of you motherless SONS A BITCHS again; it will be your heads that Jazon is holding." Ajay yelled. "Now leave."

The mercs; who were clearly terrified did not have to be asked twice; they grabbed their gear and high tailed it out of there. Only the bald man stayed behind. Jazon looked at him with opened curiosity.

SHANE

"I stayed to bury the dead and make restitution for my misdeeds." The short bald fellow said.

"Very well; I will find a few hands to help you with that; when you are finished come find me and we will discuss your future..." Jazon said

"Archie; my name is Archie Flint; I just want my name on the stone." Archie said.

Archie turned and bent his back to his work; for a soft-looking little bald man Archie worked his ass off without complaint or any breaks; until the field was cleaned up and the dead buried or taken away to be identified. Ajay who was feeling much better watched Archie; partly because he thought Collin's people were going to kill him and partly because the man seemed to be an honest man who was down on his luck and desperate not to stop trying to live. Yes, Archie made a huge blunder; but he stayed behind to make it right. Moreover, Archie had not to anyone's knowledge killed or even shot at anyone; he was basically innocent of any crimes other than stupidity.

"You know that boy thinks you are going to kill him." Ajay told Jazon.

"I know, but I am not going too." Jazon answered.

After the battle Jc pulled Terry off to the ER to pull the bullets out of him and get him patched up. Terry would only go when the mercs were all gone and he followed them passed Collin's lands to make sure they

SHANE

were not coming back. Jc was right behind him the entire time. Terry stomped to the manor house but he was to big to go into the halls, so he wolfed down and nearly fell flat from blood loss. Terry was so messed up Jc was as close to panic as he could show. Terry was the only real family as Jc had. Jc liked Jazon and Ajay but they were not wolves and so they could never be his family. Later Jc would come to realize just how foolish that belief was; when one of them dies. Jc grabbed Terry as the boy began to fall and rushed him into the ER room. Collin was sitting by the door and Kelli was black eyed and snarling at him. Kelli saw Jc and zipped forward to stop so suddenly that she toppled forward in horror. Her black eyes turned soft and blue-green again. Kelli got off the floor and pointed to the bed; that she had already put new linen on. Jc placed Terry on the bed and stepped back out of Kelli's way. She was crying and her hands shook.

"What happened to my boy? Oh you are in so much pain; are you going to die?" Kelli said frantic.

"No I am not going to die." Terry managed to say.

"You're not just saying that...are you?" Kelli seemed tiny and breakable suddenly.

   Two huge strong hands settled on her delicate shoulders and softly but firmly squeezed. Kelli looked up and Jc smiled; however it was Collin who answered her question.

"Kelli my darling; it takes a great deal to kill a full werewolf; more actually than to kill a vampire. That is

SHANE

why in all the world only Werewolves can stand against vampires and hope to win; they are as you said our nature opposite; a check to our balance. I believe this young man is even considered special even among his own pack." Collin said.

Collin looked at Jazon and Ajay; and then he looked at Jc. The lord of the manor faced Jazon and smiled.

"I dare say every member of you group is quite special; are they not. Your shadow is fearless and strong as a young bull. You wolf guardians are both bigger and more powerful than any werewolves I have ever heard of; and more you lead them by their consent; not their obedience. You are a curious fellow young hunter." Collin said.

"Shag that lot Collin; my boy is dying; do something." Kelli screamed at him.

"Be calm little sister; Terry is closer to a true immortal than anyone but Jazon, these scratches will be gone by tomorrow if he rests and eats well." Jc said calmly.

"Baby they would never let me die; you don't know it yet; but these are my family and every one of them would kill or die for me without a second thought." Terry said after spitting blood in the sink from across the room.

"How could you know that?" Kelli said with tear rolling down her fine featured face.

SHANE

"Because they already have." Terry said closing his eyes.

"TERRY!"

"I am sleepy; not dying. When I wake up I am going to need a lot of food." Terry said.

"What kind of food?" Collin asked.

"MEAT." The boys all said together and then they all laughed deeply.

Jc cleaned and dressed Terry's wounds; after he removed more than a hundred rounds from Terry. Jc told Kelli she could crawl in bed with Terry; but after she dug the bullets out of him. Kelli never really looked at Jc before. He was bigger than Terry and older. He had thick dark hair and soulful eyes; and currently he was covered in wounds of every type. How foolish Kelli felt; she could feel the draw toward Jc that she felt toward Terry. It was not sexual or love; it was more like belonging to a family; it felt right.

"Strip wolf boy; let's get those bullet out and you stitched up." Kelli said.

"When you remove the lead; the holes will close by themselves; stitches are not necessary baby sis." Jc said softly.

Kelli spent three quarters of an hour digging out bullet and pieces of stone; that Jc said were cause by grenades going off by him. Jc never moved as she cut

SHANE

and dug for the metals and stone, he just told her if there was more in any area that needed to be removed. Kelli had never seen such quiet strength; Jc was obviously tired and suffering from massive blood loss and pain; yet he acted like he was just chilling and enjoying the day.

SHANE

SHANE

CHAPTER 7: THE WILD TIME

Kelli finished up the first aid Jc needed and then she washed the blood off of his back and her hands. Jc was about to leave and Kelli stopped him.

"What is the wild time?" Kelli asked.

Jc actually looked ill for a moment; then he looked at the sleeping Terry and cleared his throat.

"I think it is best to let Terry explain tomorrow; however, I will tell you this. You are forbidden to hunt or eat anything that has raw blood on it. Listen careful now; you must never attack or kill a human; therefore for now avoid all humans unless Terry, Jazon, Collin or myself are with you." Jc said and he turned and left quickly.

Jc returned fifteen minutes and set a tray of cooked food down and a pitcher of wine. Jc smiled at Kelli and looked at Terry like a father would an ill child and then he left.

Kelli walked over and looked at the food, it was all very fine and proper; however she did not want any of it. She wanted; strangely enough to go hunt and kill her own food; like a real wolf would. Kelli was shocked by this; because she was a tender hearted young woman who was filled with love and giving. Kelli looked at her Boy; but no; that is not right; Terry was her mate. Kelli and Terry are a match set. Kelli crawled into the bed next to him and his muscular arm wrapped around her automatically even in his sleep. For the first time since she was nearly killed; and then turned into a werewolf; Kelli felt content and happy. Kelli closed her eyes with her face in the space between Terry's neck and his wide shoulder; and she slept happily.

Down the hall Jc was having a serious conversation with Jazon and Collin. Ajay listened silently; because Jc told him that the task at hand was not appointed to him and he might die if he interferes. Ajay knew that Jc was not threatening him; rather he was stating the facts plainly as usual. Jc was trying to explain the danger and for some reason Collin was being an ass; and he was purposely not getting the Gist of it.

"Listen up jackass; if Kelli gets near a human in the next two days or an animal; she will rip them apart and eat them raw. I know you're not a wolf, but you have lived long enough to know how dangerous an insane werewolf can be. When we have one of those; then we hunt them down and destroy them; because they can not be saved once they given in to the feral beast within. We are no longer the monsters we were when you were young Collin." Jc said slowly for effect.

"It is settled then; until Kelli is able to withstand the wild drive within her; we will take turns guarding her. If we fail then we will have to kill her; which means we will have to kill Terry as well. I am not willing to do either of those things right now." Jazon said.

"I do not see why this is our problem?" Collin said.

SHANE

Jc looked angry on a level that his friends had never seen before when he turned his eyes to Collin. The words he said shocked all three of them to the bone.

"Collin I was around when you were born; it was I who took you from the vampire who killed you human family and bite you as well. I killed him and saved you. I took you to Sven to be raised and explain what you were and why you must be protected. You are not the last of you family Collin O'Day. Now, you will help keep that girl alive and well; if you ever loved her stop pushing her away; she needs you now." Jc said in a low tone. "Ajay nothing personal; but she would kill you if you tried to help".

"No problem man, I am dead tired and all beat up; I can use some down time." Ajay said.

When the sun went down and the moon rose into the sky the great ivory Goddess of the night, Kelli began to have a beautiful dream. Kelli was wondering through the hall of O'Day manor and the moon light made her feel whole and powerful; and she liked it. Suddenly, from behind Kelli there was the sound of padded feet and claws on the marble floors. At first Kelli was only curious; but as the sound grew closer; she was less interested and more nervous. Kelli began to walk away at the quick step as those in the army say. The sound of strong feet still grew louder and more determined to follow her. Kelli lost it and broke into a desperate run; it made no difference; the feet just matched her pace and then some. Kelli was no coward because she was the adopted daughter of a powerful vampire; however, Collin was not here to protect her. Kelli was drenched

SHANE

with sweat and was breathing hard and shallow. Kelli was spent; she could not get away so she turned and screamed.

"SHOW YOURSELF!"

From the depths of the moon lit halls came a great soft red haired beast. The eyes were as black as the deepest pools of oil, the teeth were long daggers of death and saliva was dripping off of them. The beast moved fast but completely silent. It ran right up to Kelli and lowered it's huge head until their eyes were at the same level. In those eyes Kelli saw only death and pain. Kelli was no longer afraid; she reached forward and touched the beast's huge snarling maw and leaned her head against it's head.

"It is okay; you will never be alone again; we will face this life together." Kelli said.

In the instant that Kelli accepted the beast in her heart; she became one with it and was running faster than she could have ever imagined through the woods and then the open fields. The freedom of the wind kissing her body lovingly was a sensation that bordered on erotic. In that moment Kelli finally let go and then it happened. The dream changed and the feeling of freedom became instead a prison. There was a horrible pain so horrible that Kelli screamed and cried. Kelli finally opened her eyes ending the dream; and Kelli was shocked at what she saw.

"Stay calm and don't move little sister." Jc said.

"Okay." Kelli said in a shaky voice.

Jc seemed surprised to hear her voice; at the least he was amused. Kelli looked passed him and Collin was laying on his side bleeding profusely from deep claw marks. Jazon was standing over him; speaking in a low tone. Kelli thought Jazon attacked Collin and she got mad. She tried to get up; but Jc slammed her flat again hard with a stern look on his face. That was when Kelli saw that Jc was ripped up as well and bleeding. Jc saw the confusion in her eyes and was going to say something but Kelli spoke first.

"Damn you let me up; the bastard is attacking my father!" Kelli screamed.

Jazon looked at Kelli; his eyes were white and glowing. Jc was loosening his grip on Kelli; she thought it was to let her up; she was wrong. Jc jerked her to her feet in a grip so powerful; she felt like her bone would crumble in it.

"Look again Kelli; Jazon is offering his rich blood to Collin to heal him. It was not Jazon who ripped Collin and me up." Jc said.

"What; who in the hell could beat you two up except Jazon who is the most powerful person I have even met?" Kelli said.

Kelli's head snapped around in the direction of Terry in utter panic. Terry was sound asleep and in the bed looking much better than when Kelli fell asleep in his arms.

SHANE

"Who do you think did all of this baby sis?" Jc asked amused again.

"How would I know; I wake up and your pinning me to the floor like an animal...."Kelli said and then gasped.

"Yes, now you understand baby sister; this is the wild times; and this is why you can't be around humans or animals, you will slaughter them on instinct. That will stop once you come to grips with your inner wolf." Jc said.

Jc turned to Collin and smiled; but it was not a nice smile at all.

"So still think it is not important to have a powerful guardian watching her? Not feeling to damn smart now are you babe?" Jc pressed him.

"It was only my pride that was injured dog; I will heal and I will never forget the thrashing my once tiny little daughter gave me in her sleep." Collin answered.

Terry woke up and looked at Kelli.

"Come'ere baby." Terry said to Kelli.

Kelli tossed Jc like a feather in the wind out of her way to go to Terry. Terry saw his wee girl toss his large powerful friend like a old shoe out of her way. He giggled at Kelli. She literally jumped into his arms pouting up at him.

"Wow you are quite a little destroyer." Terry said looking at the damage to the metal door and Collin; and then he looked at Jc and saw he was clawed up as well.

"Don't tease me; this is all new to me. I was having a beautiful dream about a great sad beast and then we ran together and I was such a joy Terry. I woke up with Jc slamming me into the floor." Kelli said.

"WHAT?" Terry snarled.

"Oh shit." Jazon said.

Jc was thrown through the wall in less than a blink of an eye; before he landed Terry was standing over him like an avenging angel. Now Jc is a bad man and not someone you wanted to cross lightly; however at this moment he can hear the bells of St Mary's ringing and knew if he decide to fight Terry might kill him in anger. So, Jc decided to explain.

"Nice throw Ter. Now listen to me for a second; before this gets way out of hand. Collin was guarding the door and I heard a huge crash and then I could hear screams of pain and agony. I ran down here to find baby sis beating the stuffing out of big daddy Collin; with eyes as black as coal stones and she was out of her mind. It was only the fact that Collin had a hold of her ankle that kept her from running down the hall and killing everyone." Jc said.

"Okay, how do you know she was out of control/" Terry said.

SHANE

Jc was now pissed off; he kicked Terry in the chest launching him on to his back. Jc jumped up and walked over to his friend and growled at him.

"I yelled her name; I let her claw me up while I shook her; trying to get her to focus on the present and she would not. She was lost in the grip of the beast brother; and you know damn well what that means." Jc said sternly.

Terry got up and looked Jc in the eye; there was a very clear understanding that passed between them; but it did not need to be said. They walked together back to Kelli who was starting to shake badly; she looked like a druggy who was coming down hard after a big extended high. Jazon had her cornered. Kelli was bleeding from her lower lip. Terry started to inflate; but he stopped when Jazon turned his eyes on Terry.

"If you are foolish enough to take a crack at me Terry; I will not hold back; and you will smart for it." Jazon said in a dangerous tone that made both wolves step back in caution. "Kelli is hurting right now; and her blood smells all wrong to me; is what is happening now normal?"

Terry stepped far around Jazon and walked over to Kelli; her eyes went from black back to light aqua.

"Terry back away from her." Jazon ordered.

Terry was about to defy Jazon; but he thought better of it; Jazon was their leader and he was strong and loyal to his boys. Terry backed up five steps and Jc gasped.

"Oh for God sake; look at that." Jc said

Terry saw plain as day what Jc was surprised about. Kelli's eyes went black when he was out of a short range from her; and she became feral. However, Kelli was her sweet gentle self when Terry was near her; which should not matter during her wild times. Jazon had seen enough. He took off his belt and walked over to Terry and pushed him up to Kelli.

"Hold hands you two." Jazon said.

The young lovers did as they were told happily. Jazon stepped forward and wrapped his belt around their hands and buckled it. He touched Terry's shoulder.

"Come on let's go sit in the parlor and watch the sun come up." Jazon said.

"Ah, Jazon are you sure?" Jc asked.

"Yes, besides this place is trashed and we need to let Collin's people in here to fix this junk; and we need to talk Kelli's new life over." Jazon explained.

They all went to the sitting room by the kitchen and watched the sun come up once more. Food was brought to them to enjoy; Collin who joined them after changing his attire was more than a little shocked to see Kelli sitting on the mini couch with Terry snuggling. Collin remained silent about it. Terry saw him looking them over and it was beginning to irritate him.

SHANE

"What is it Sir Collin; you are staring daggers through us; and frankly it is bothering me; so speak your mind." Terry said sharply.

Collin did indeed have a sour face for Terry; but it was for only Terry and not Kelli.

"I did not know you were going to turn my beautiful daughter into a monstrous beast; who is out of her mind. Frankly, you disgust me mongrel." Collin said,

Terry had his off hand already undoing the belt on his arm and was rising to likely kill Collin. Fast as a humming bird Jazon had one hand on Terry's should sitting him back against the couch and the other hand over the buckle on belt. Terry looked into Jazon's eyes and saw only friendship; not one ounce of anger. Jazon smiled at him.

"Relax brother puppy; Collin just got his booty handed to him by the little slip of a girl belted to you; his pride is sore and so not doubt are other parts of him. Besides, it is not good for you and Kelli to be parted. Kelli gets...peckish." Jazon said with a knowing smile.

"You know I am hungry; may I have a cookie shadow?" Kelli said to Ajay.

"Sure, take one." Ajay said as he held the plate out to her to take a cookie.

Kelli nibbled delicately on the cookie until it was gone; and then she drank some tea and had another cookie. The boys talked about a lot of things; but they stopped when Kelli reached for the belt and undid the buckle and stood. Jazon was about to react, Collin was already on his feet. Jc did nothing to get up; but he put things into perspective.

"It is all good, let her be." Jc said.

"Good, because these cookies are no where near as good as mine; so I am off to the kitchen to make you some good ones." Kelli announced.

The pretty young girl turned kissed Collin on the cheek and whispered in his ear.

"I love you and I am sorry for the troubles I have caused." Kelli said, and then she slipped away.

Everyone heard what she said except Ajay; because she is a pure human. Collin and Jazon looked a bit more apprehensive about letting Kelli go unattended. Jc smiled at Jazon.

"How do you know she is not going to go all nutters?" Collin asked.

Jc smiled at the lord of the castle and Terry laughed right out loud. There was some inside joke they were enjoying.

"Kelli ate human food and drank tea." Jc said.

"So what does that matter?" Collin bellowed.

SHANE

"Because she was not offered Collin; she asked for it and enjoyed eating the food. It did not taste like ashes in her mouth. When she chose human food to satisfy her inner need and when she said she could make better; she made the final change. Kelli is a head of normal schedule for the wild times, and they are not over; she will still be dangerous during the night; however as long as the sun is up and nobody tries to make her angry; Kelli is safe enough. (Jc grinned at Terry) I might add that if anything makes Kelli's blood rise Terry will know; they are irreversibly linked for life." Jc explained.

Ajay tossed a cook to Terry and smiled. Terry blushed a little bit; Ajay seemed like a wise uncle to him and Terry found he very much wanted Ajay to approve of him; every since Ajay had helped save his life in the old coliseum or sports stadium. Terry did not know anyone who was braver and more loyal than Ajay. Between Jazon and Ajay no foe was their match, and no task was too large and no life they would not try to save, they were blessed and curse in Terry's view.

"Guess our puppy is a full grown dog now; she is a lovely girl. I hope you can handle her kid." Ajay said.

By the time Kelli returned with a fresh stack of hot cookies; the boys stopped worrying about her and their minds went back tot the quest at hand; saving Silky. Ajay went back to his silent mode, he was deeply disturbed by the fact that he had failed and his girl way dying. Jazon understood how he felt this was really his trip; Jazon and the wolves came to support Ajay's play and back him up if it all went south.

SHANE

"How does this Silky girl have to live?" Kelli asked.

Terry and Jc held their breath and gave Kelli a be careful look and then looked pointedly at Ajay.

"I did not mean it the way it sounded Shadow; I don't know her and I only wanted to get a working idea of how long we have to find and beat the answers out of Brian Finney? I ask your pardon for my thoughtless words." Kelli said.
"You are a sweet kid and I was not offended. I sadly don't know if Silky is dead or I have more time. Damn it all I just don't know." Ajay said.

"We could form a plan if we knew where the black heart went." Collin said.

(Laugh)

All eyes turned to Jazon who was smiling like a poor kid with a hundred dollar bill he just found on the ground. Jazon elbowed Ajay hard.

"We do know." Jazon said.

To answer the obvious questions; Jazon put Mark's cell phone and his train and plane tickets on the table they were sitting around nibbling on cookies.

"Oh man." Terry said.

"Excellent." Jc exclaimed.

SHANE

"I feel like such an ass. I took these off Mark dead butt and then we had a few issues that came up and I put these items out of my mind until we could deal with the current dangers. I called Jax two hours ago. Biz and Silky have a weird link in their minds, so Silky is speaking thru Biz, she is fine. Pegi and Tad have used magic and potions to keep the poison from taking a grip on Silky. She will not die before you return; Silky herself said this. She is okay for now; she just can not wake up. So, little big brother let's go find Brian and beat the after life out of him." Jazon said in a hard tone.

"Are you all going to leave?" Payton asked as he suddenly walked in.

Connor was standing right beside him; however he was looking at Collin. Collin looked back at the wily assassin-theft and knew the question in his mind. They had made a deal; however, that was before Connor was aware his brother was not dead. Further, Payton was a member of Jazon's crew; so it was complicated. On the one hand both of the boys were cold blooded killers; without any restrain I might add; and more important; they were fearless to the extreme. They had proved that when they hunted vampires with only blades and had managed to kill everyone of their prey. Other the other hand they were just boys and that was no kind of life for them. If there was a third hand it would be; these boys because of their success killing vampires were already marked for death. Collin was not sure if he should ask them to stay or encourage them to go with the heroes; yes, Collin finally admitted it to himself; that is what these people were; they were heroes.

SHANE

"Yes P, we are leaving; we have to find Brian to save Silky's life. It is up to you whether you come along or stay here with Collin; who I am positive would be very happy if you chose that avenue. I think I would not be out of line if I said; you are one of us; we have fought and lived through battles together; we have laughed and cried out in pain together and still we have endured. You are our brother in everything but blood; except with Jazon; where blood was involved." Terry said.

"What about Connor?" Payton asked.

"He is welcome to come along with us as well; we will give him the opportunity to earn our trust just as you have. Your blood is our blood littlest brother." Jc said.

The other members of the crew all nodded in agreement. Collin was beside himself; he wanted to say something very badly; and he seemed sad in a deep way.

"Will you take Kelli as well; when you leave? I have a closet full of questions for Jc about my past and his. I also do not condone going after the families of an enemy because you are to weak to beat you opponent; therefore, gentlemen I am going to help you as must as I can. You have made a powerful friend in me; and a loyal one as well. I have a feeling that the young men will be following along with you. I want to know what you intend to do with them when you go back to America?" Collin asked.

SHANE

Jc looked at Collin and made a hard face that looked like he was insulted. Jazon smiled and winked at Ajay; Ajay smiled. Terry was plainly miffed at the abrasive question.

"We thought we would dump them in what ever city we were in when we decide to go home." Jc paused for effect; clearly insulted.

"What else Collin; we are taking them home with us. We have a huge hotel resort and an army of magical folks to teach the boys and train them to be more than they are. Their lives will be their own always, but they will always have a giant family to lean on...if the need arises." Jazon said good naturedly.

"Oh, I see." Collin answered.

SHANE

CHAPTER 8: SILKY'S SURPRISE.

A few days after Alister came over and had a amazing meal with Pegi and Jax as hostesses; Block started to vibrate. I do not mean he shook a little like a person with Parkinson's disease; I mean he shook like there was an earthquake happening inside of his body. Tad who was close to him seemed to know something but would not share; for that matter neither did any of the elves. Block did not get grumpy or mean; and he held the little one as he walked because his new vibration made them laugh; and Block loved the sounds of laughter, especially children's laughter. The smell of hot apple pie increased ten fold with Block's new shaking; it was pleasant.

Biz who rarely left Silky's side except when Pegi and Jax bathed her; saw Silky's eyes twitch at the same time that Block's apple pie smell increased. Biz spoke softly into Silky's mind and her answer made him frantic to find Jax. Jax was not sleeping; she had horrible dreams about a slaughter on a train and a siege of a castle. These were stupid dreams; nobody lay siege to a castle anymore. Jax had called Jazon in tears; and then she told him everything she saw in her dreams. He told her that everything she saw actually did happen. Jazon told her that they all lived and they even increased the members of their crew to plus three. One very attractive girl; Terry's mate, and two brothers; who might be the best pure hand to eye coordinated knife jocks who ever lived; they were superhuman at it; Jazon told Jax. He also told Jax how miserable Ajay was and

SHANE

that Mark was caught and beaten by Ajay near death; however the final blow was leveled by Collin O'Day the lord of all of Europe. Consequently, Collin was Mark grand father. Jazon ended the call with how much he loved her and that his heart was sore from the lack of her warm body next to his. Jax cried happy tears after that. Anyway, like I said Jax was not sleeping well; so Biz hated to wake her. But he did. Biz went up to Jax's door and knocked firmly. Jax did not like it when you tapped; she wanted a hard knock like you had a pair.

"Whaaa; go away I mmm sweeping!" Jax hollered more than half asleep.

Biz hit the door with a little more power and the walls shook. Jax jumped out of bed in just a baby-doll tee and her thong; she ripped the door open and there was Biz. Jax's heart fell; she thought that if Biz was here that meant Silky was dead or dieing. Biz blushed a little because Jax was nearly naked and she was extremely hot. Biz wrote a note on his pad and showed it to Jax. (Silky is fine... and so are you, wink, wink. Sadly you should get dressed and come with me). Jax read the note and smiled; she pulled Biz into her arms and hugged him and then kissed his cheek.

"You are a very sweet man Biz; I hope you find a woman who truly deserves you someday." Jax said.

Jax turned ripped her tee-shirt off and then turned back to Biz. He was staring at her nude breasts smiling. She smiled and then kicked the door shut as an after thought. Jax opened the door a few moments later and smiled at Biz. Together they walked down to Silky's

SHANE

room, she was tossing and turning. Jax was concerned; but Biz held her back and he pointed at his eyes and then at Silky. Jax got that he wanted her to just watch; so that is exactly what she did. Silky tossed a little more and then she began to mumble. They could not make out her words but she was trying to speak desperately.

"How long do we just watch?" Jax asked.

Biz made a pinching motion with his thumb and index finger; mean just a bit more. He was of-course bizarrely linked to Silky' which nobody understood; not even him. Then Silky said her first discernable words.

"Damn it!" Silky blurted.

"Okay she seems pissed; is that a good sign or a bad one?" Jax asked.

Biz smiled so wide and handsome; that Jax grabbed his hand and squeezed it. He pulled Jax to the bed and touched Silky with Jax's left hand. Silky opened her eyes and smiled back. Silky was covered in sweet.

"Hello pretty, pretty." Silky said to Jax.

"Hello baby girl." Jax said with wee tears on the edges of her eyes.

Silky looked at Biz and smiled at him.

"My lovely boy; my link; my key to the prison I have been in. I love you Biz...and thank you for

SHANE

everything...both of you." Silky said as she looked from Biz to Jax.

Silky tried to get up but she was dizzy and weak; so Biz walked over and easily lifted her right off the bed. Silky looked into his eyes; Biz nodded and left by the door; Jax followed them down the stairs. A few people looked to see what was happening. It was not until a faerie saw Silky's eyes open that Pegi was told. Pegi came bursting into the huge reception hall to find Silky sitting on Biz's lap chatting with Wolf and Enoch. Pegi started crying because she deep down believed Silky was dying and eventually Ajay was going to come home and it was Pegi that would have to face him with the news. Yet, here was her wood nymph friend sitting up and talking; although in short measured spurts. Silky was extremely tired; so she did not blather on much. Biz held her like a small child in his powerful arms. Biz was not a big guy; but the fact he shared a body with a fire demon (a redeemed soul; good guy) made Biz powerful and immortal. Biz loved Silky, she was his closest friend; I don't know who was more tore up when Silky went into a coma: Ajay or Biz.

"Pegi came here and give me some sugar baby; while I am able to stay awake." Silky said.

Pegi rushed over to her and held her close; there were tears and laughter; there was also concern. Silky was burning up still. Pegi finally let go of Silky and promptly told a faerie to fetch her red-brown earthen jug. The faeries who loved Pegi; jumped to do as she always kindly asked. When the jug was in Pegi's hand she, grabbed a glass and pour some of the honey colored liquid in the glass and gave it to Silky. The nymph smelled it; and of-course it smelled great; everything Pegi made smelled great. Silky drank it and immediately looked better and her temp dropped.

"How did you wake up?" Tad asked concerned that this could be a super bad sign.

"I smelled apple pie and my head began to spin and suddenly I could see light outside my eyelids and I was able to mumble. I tried to speak and move until Jax came and then I woke up." Silky explained.

Tad's tiny face went chalk white and his eyes bulged out.

"BLOCK!" Tad screamed at the top of his lungs.

The shaking ancient troll walked in carrying children. Almost by magic Silky jumped up and ran across to Block and flung herself into his mighty tree trunk sized arms. Silky looked vibrant as soon as she was close to Block. Tad looked ill. Pegi noticed and asked what the matter was.

"Later, not now Pegi." Tad explained.

"Okay; but as soon as possible." Pegi said softly; yet firmly.

The rest of the day was spent with Silky staying right beside Block; and Biz staying right beside Silky. Father Sully and John Bishop came right away to see Silky. Mick was overjoyed that the gentle girl was

SHANE

looking better and awake. John had never met a wood nymph before and was enchanted by her easy loving ways.

"You are so sweet and caring Silky." John said.
"When you are an earth girl you have to learn to love the world around you; to help it grow and flourish. I seem to have a deep well of love to share thank God." Silky said.

"I am constantly in awe of you folks; I was so hopelessly under educated about the history of the world. We are taught that magical creatures are all these mean evil people. That is complete garbage; you folks are among the nicest people I have ever known and by far as a group the most caring. It has been delightful to meet you Silky." John said.

"The pleasure has been all of mine kind sir." Silky giggled.

Tad saw Jax reach for her cell phone; fast as a cobra, Tad pitched a quarter and knocked it out of her hand. Jax looked at him and he waved her over. Jax came; tad turned and led her and Pegi who he popped in the butt away to another room quickly. When all three of them were in the room; Tad closed and locked the door. Tad raised his hands and spoke four ancient words. Pegi understood what he said and was instantly alert; Jax had no idea.

"I have sealed the room not to keep you gals in; but to keep any prying eyes and ears out. What I am about to tell you two is in the strictest confidence; it is a closely guarded secret. Block has agreed to let me tell you

SHANE

since Silky is involved. By the bye Jax; I apologize for throwing a coin at you. I could not let you call Jazon or Ajay about Silky until you know the truth." Tad said in a miserable voice.

"Say your piece Tad; we will listen to you with open hearts and open minds." Pegi recited the elf pledge of learning; which was a powerful magic unto itself.

Jax just nodded that she agreed. Tad took a seriously deep breath like he did not want to have to say what was coming. He let out his breath and deflated more than either woman had ever seen the irrepressible Gnome become. Tad sat on one of the chairs and hung his head.

"It is an old story that I must tell; so bear with me ladies. As you know Block is very special on many levels. Well, he is much more than that. Many centuries ago Block was like many trolls; he was hateful at the treatment mankind and other beings gave him because of his looks. He was a mighty warrior and my own enemy. (Tad paused here and looked at both women). Block was an unstoppable juggernaut, no gnome or even elf could hope to stop him in battle. We tried everything to kill him. We burned him; stabbed him; we blew him up; we tried to drown him; and nothing, I tell you nothing can kill Block. One day during the most bloody horrible battle in the history of the world; I found myself mortally injured and at Blocks mercy. I knew I was dead and not by his hands. I called out to him to finish me; he came to me and I spoke with him for the first time.

SHANE

"Mighty troll come to me." Tad said.

"What do you want of me; gnome who is dying?" Block said.

"I don't want to die alone and forgotten." Tad explained.

"I am your enemy little one; I should just leave you to your fate." Block said plainly.

"Then just finish me off before you leave." Tad told Block.

The troll stood up to his full height and looked at Tad. The little brawny gnome was ready to be killed and did not expect anything more from the troll but this final kindness. However Tad was wrong; he was not ready to die or be killed. When Block stood there looking at Tad without doing anything the gnome grew angry as his life leaked away into the earth.

Tad stopped his story for a moment and he had tears on his rugged face. He gathered himself for a few moments and then he plodded on.

"I did something that has been the black stain on my soul for my entire life since." Tad explained.

Block looked down at the down at the little fellow with an odd look on his face just as Tad spoke in a low harsh voice.

"Troll I curse you to never die; and you will be able to only serve the enemies you once slew from this date until forever." Tad growled.

Tad looked ill as he continued.

"Well I curse Block ad he took it all wrong. The troll looked at me and laughed. He reached down with his giant hands and picked me up and turned and began to leave. I asked him what he was doing. Block just laughed and kept going. When he final spoke this is what he said." Tad said

"I have always just wanted to be friends with the world at large; I never wanted to hurt anyone. Your curse has set me free little gnome: and it has saved your life as well. I will not let my liberator die. I have a secret that I have never shared; not even with my fellow trolls. My skin contains the most powerful curative in the world." Block said.

Block took me back to his camp and told all the troll army to stand down; but not to let anyone come into the camp for one full day. Block was obeyed to the letter. The entire Gnome and elf armies were told by envoy that the trolls did not want to continue the current battle and if they would wait for one full day; Block himself would address them on the terms for ending the war. The elves and the gnomes and our allies were glad of this; because to be honest the troll were handing us our butts pretty handily. Block was by my side the entire time; as were one gnome girl: at first I though she was a slave or a prisoner; but I realized that was wrong when Block tossed her up and down and she

SHANE

laughed freely. The girl was young; younger than me at the time and I was forty-six; which is still considered a child. If not for my combat ability and arcane skills; I would never have been near a battle field; however, my talents were greater than anyone at the time older then myself; so I was made an officer and sent to war. I was scared for the girl; but she was completely at ease with the giant leader of the trolls. She took a sharp knife out and used it to scrape Block's arm; she collected the scrapings and put them to boiling in water. Within moments the tent smelled of fresh apple pie; I breathed deeply thinking it was a delusion and I was dying. Well, I began to feel better almost immediately; and then the girl took some of the water from the pot and washed my wounds with it. Like a miracle they began to close almost instantly; when all of Tad's injuries looked well along in their healing the troll got up from the corner where he sat quietly and tossed the boiling water out of the tent and he returned with fresh water and two clean towels, the girl washed me again. I was confused so I asked; what was the reason for all of this. The leader of the trolls smiled and regarded me as a guest and a friend rather than a recent enemy.

"I have healed you to a point where your injuries could not kill you any longer, but only to that point; if I continued it could have a counter effect on you and I would not want that; my little friend." Block explained.

Tad sat there looking at the girls; without saying anything. Pegi was intrigued with the tale and wanted to hear more. Jax seemed to be getting part of what tad was telling but she let Pegi prod Tad for more.

SHANE

"Well what happened then?" Pegi said.

"I got better in one day and Block brought me out of the tent fully armed with my weapons. The Gnome army cheered because they thought I was lost among the dead. Block walked behind me and let me go and do as I saw fit to do." Tad said. "When I got up to our general; I explained my story and he looked at Block; who struck fear in the hearts of his foes. Blocked waited for me to finish and then he spoke."

"I never wanted this war; I only wanted to be met with peace and friendship; not swords and spears. Tad is now my brother and as such I am his protector; his enemies are my own. I have but one demand; and it will be met or else the war will continue until you are no more." Block let his voice rise like thunder.

The gnome-elf armies took a step back in fear; but not Tad; he remained rooted to his place without any hint of fear or regret.

"Tell them your demand Block; and they will listen to it; for they are wise and good of heart." Tad said.

"My demand is that troll hunting is no longer tolerated or encouraged. We are a peaceful people by nature; despite our appearance. If we are attacked and killed because we are troll just one single time more. I will see to it the offending person and their entire race is wiped out to the life. This is my word and my bond. Know this I can not be killed or injured by any means you know of; so as long as I am alive I will finish what I

SHANE

have started ...always." Block said in a booming stern tone.

A single elf warrior priest stepped forward and addressed Block without the slightest fear.

"I speak for all the elves on this world; and I give my word that not a single one of my race will break you treaty of peace; if they do than they are not an elf any longer; they are prey and I will hunt them as animals. Now, I give you my oath Troll king; if a single member of the faerie folk are killed by a troll and it was not self defense; than that troll and only that troll is subject to my justice. If any troll tries to interfere I will kill them as well. You have the word of Kalesar." The elf said equally sternly.

There was a rumble among the trolls; Kalesar was known to all as the indestructible elf. He was Block's match and no elf would disobey him. Block laughed and then he held out his hand to the elf; Kal looked at it skeptically; so Block got down on his knee and reached out again. The elf surprised everyone by laughing and dropping to his knees as well; and he shook Blocks hand firmly.

"The three of us have been close every since that day; we have been challenge over the years to wars and we always won them and showed the young a better road to travel." Tad ended his story.

Pegi looked at Tad and then at Jax. Jax knew what she was going to say; however she waited for Pegi to put it to words. Jax knew that Silky's miracle wake up had to do with Block but there was still something missing here.

"Tad, tie Silky into the story we just listened to please." Pegi asked.

"Block is shedding so to speak; you know how hard his body is; so think rocks grinding on rocks. When Block sheds part of the hide is airborne dust; because of how it comes off of him. Everyone is inhaling it right now." Tad explained.

"Should we be worried about the over effects it can have then; are we in danger?" Pegi asked.

"No, no, we are all fine; if you have a minor health issue; then after inhaling Block's dust you don't anymore." Tad said.

"However, Silky was dying from a rare and unknown poison; so she could get an overdoes and become worse than if she was to begin with." Jax guessed.

"Yes, that is the worry. We need to get Silky out of here today, just in case." Tad said.

Pegi looked at Tad and spoke sharply too him.

"What is the rest of it gnome; I can see there is more to the story than we were told?" Pegi said.

Tad gave Pegi a hard look; but he did not say anything. However Jax did.

SHANE

"Block is in danger as well isn't he?" Jax asked.

Before Tad could answer the door glowed and then it opened. Standing by the door was Kal and Block.

"May we come in?" Kal asked.

"Yes of-course." Pegi said.

The troll and the elf came in. The elf re-sealed the door with magic that overlapped the magic Tad had performed. Block just leaned back against the door. It would take a dragon to move him if he did not want to move. Jax looked confused; so Pegi explained.

"The elf had a pass-key, a bypass to Tad's magic' so they could enter without interrupting the seal; and then Kalesar placed his own seal over the top to make it even more impossible to enter or listen in on our conversations." Pegi said.

"Very good witch; you have a deep understanding of the arcane ways." Kal said.

"My father was an elf like you Kal; he was a powerful magic user and he taught me. My mother was a human earth witch; she was one with nature and taught me those ways as well." Pegi explained.

"I should like to discuss your powers and knowledge one day soon." Kal replied.

"What is the rest of the story with you Block? Tad told us about the healing potential of your hide and the

SHANE

airborne dust; but there is more isn't there?" Jax asked deftly.

"Yes, I shed like am doing once every two hundred years; and for two or three days I am vulnerable to harm. Only the people in this room know this and no other. So, my life is now in your hands ladies." Block said.

Jax startled the giant troll by laughing at him and then sitting on his lap. The room looked at her like she lost her mind. Jax wiped the tears from her eyes and explained.

"You big dummy; I can be killed everyday in a million ways; and I am getting older every second. I know your not afraid Block; but you should know that most of us know the grip of our mortality every second of our short ass lives and we endure it. I will never tell your secret to anyone; not even my own true love Jazon. It is your secret and you are my friend. I will do my part to protect you this time; because you protect us the rest of the time." Jax kissed his giant nose and stood up. "We have to get Silky out of here for the next few days."

"No, I am going to the vault when I leave here; it is air tight and I will stay there until Kal or Tad comes for me. Silky will be fine; however she will go back to sleep soon after I sequester myself. Visit with her and enjoy her for now." Block was sad.

The giant troll got up and waited for the elf and gnome to drop their magic; and then he opened the door and walked out it and took a hard left to the stone

SHANE

stairs that led to the lower levels. Pegi felt sorry for him; but not because of what Block was going through; but because she knew his heart was breaking over not being able to help Silky more than he was doing now. Block was a truly good soul and his pain was always a sense of sadness to those around him. Jax practically ran to her other best friend Silky; because her best girl Pegi was hot on her butt. They found Silky and held her and talked to her about everything they could think of. In the end they called Ajay and let Silky talk to him alone until she fell back to sleep. Biz knew when Silky dropped back to sleep and he alerted Jax. Biz carried his closest friend up to his bed; so that he could sit in his antiques rocker and rock Silky in his arms while he cried. Silky's mind was still awake and his anguish was fresh between their special link and she comforted him; but her eyes cried as well.

SHANE

CHAPTER 9: KAHN

When Ajay's phone rang and he answered it; the powerful young black man nearly fell over from joy.

"Hey there baby; I just woke up and I wanted to talk to you before I fell back to sleep; maybe forever this time." Silky said.

"Oh my God Silky, how did you wake up? Did Pegi finally figure out what the poison was and how to beat it; or did Tad find some ancient magical way to wake you up?" Ajay cried.

"No baby; it was Block. His skin is shedding and it has some curative properties; that woke me." Silky said sweetly.

"Well, then your going to be ok now and I can come home right away." Ajay said all excited.

When Silky did not answer him; Ajay figured out there was a but or and coming for sure. He was right of-course.

"I can't stay near Block anymore; if I do it might OD me and I will die baby. I love you and I am not going to die with you so far away. Find Mark and beat him up until he tells you how to help me." Silky said.

"I found Mark; he did not know anything. He is dead; now we are going after Brian; alive or dead he will tell me what I want to know; and then I am coming home to you." Ajay said with tears on his obsidian face.

"How are Jazon and the wolves?" Silky asked.

"Jazon is miserable without Jax to calm him; I have rarely seen him so ruthless; it is like part of him is dying everyday we are away from home. Terry is in love and has a new mate Kelli. She is an Irish girl who was hurt and he turned her into a wolf like him; she will be coming home with Terry. Jc is miserable like Jazon. Collin, Mark's grand father is a hell of a guy; nothing like Mark at all. We also picked up a few strays; I will explain that later. Let me just say the Shadow has found his guard." Ajay said.

"I wish you boys were home; we all miss you. Even when I am asleep; my mind isn't. Biz and I can communicate telepathically; so when you come home you can still talk to me baby until..." Silky said

"You are not going to die Silky; don't ever think of that; not ever. If you die, I will follow soon after you; as long as Brian is dead." Ajay said angrily.
"Don't be mad coco puffs; I will not leave you without saying goodbye; I promise." Silky yawned and her eyes started to flutter.

Ajay could hear the exhaustion in her tiny soft voice.

"I am going to find a way to save you Silky no matter what." Ajay said.

"Sweaty promise me; if I don't make it; if I can not be saved that you will not waste your beautiful life; PROMISE ME!" Silky's voice was cracking with effort.

"I promise." Ajay whispered weakly as he began to crying unashamed.

"Good, I love you...miss ya...wan...you...in (deep breath) bed...baby...my Ajay." Silky said as she slipped into her coma again.

Jax picked up the phone; she was crying as well. Ajay could hear her heart beating even through the phone.

"Ajay, you and Jazon get the mother...(Her teeth were grinding with emotion) just get him; and come back to us alive. Do not waste your lives. Ajay you know what I mean; Jazon will fight until his own bones are dust unless you save him from himself. Bring my man home or I will never forgive you; in return I will make sure Silky is safe and comfortable and never alone; I promise. I love her too; she is me and Pegi's best friend." Jax said as she sobbed.

"I will do what I can; my word on it little girl. Here you should talk to your boy before we have to blow." Ajay said.

"Hey Ajay." Jax said.

"Yah?"

SHANE

"You are my family too; my loved brother; so you come back in one piece as well." Jax said in a shaky voice.

Ajay was choked up and could not answer; he just gave the phone to Jazon. Jazon stood there listening, his semi red eyes (the color they were as a human; before he turned in to a vampire) filled with angry tears and then just anger and resolve. Jazon said four words before he gave Ajay back the phone.

"I love you; goodbye."

Jazon's eyes were more red now and his face was hard like it was made of stone. He looked at Ajay and kept his gaze there for along time. He seemed to be thinking hard about his words and what he should say.

"Come with me brother." Jazon final said.
The long time blood brothers walked into Collin's manor house and into his private study. There was a servant there. Jazon asked for a bottle of rum or Irish whiskey, ice and two glasses. The servant left and returned with the requested items. Jazon thanked her and closed the door and locked it behind her when she left. Jazon put an ice cube in each glass and then filled both glasses full of booze. He sat facing his closest family in the world. He spoke and shocked Ajay to the bone with what he said.

"Brother, this was your quest up till we saw Mark's head hit the floor. I did not come to Europe to get Mark or Brian; to hell with the both of them. I did not come because Silky is dying. I came because if I ever let something happen to you; my only real family in the entire world; I would die of grief. I WAS here to just support you and make sure the job got done; we got the cure and you returned safely to your lover. Well, that shit is over. I am from here on out going to not only bring down Brian Finney; but the entire system that put a prick like him in power to begin with." Jazon said as he tipped up and drain his entire glass.

Ajay would have been furious if any other person said what Jazon just did; when Silky was laying in a bed dying. Ajay was not mad at all; he was sad. Ajay remembered how Jazon took on an entire army on the train alone and come close to dying; or something like that. Could Jazon die? The battle at Collin's castle jumped into his mind then unbidden. Terry and Jc ripped the entire merc army to piece and paid a terrible price in pain and misery for it just like they did on the train when they fought five to one odds. Ajay's friends were paying the price for his revenge in blood; their own blood. They did all of this to keep him safe. They let him fight Mark alone out of respect for him and brotherhood; but all the rest of the time they protected him. What a fool Ajay thought to himself; I am a fool not to see my friend killing themselves to save my worthless ass. Ajay looked into Jazon's burning eyes.

"BULLSHIT!"

"What?"

"I can read your face bro; you know I could always look into your heart. All that we did; was to survive; for all of us to survive. We did not pull you out of harms way, you did your part the same as we all did. We are all in it to win it bro. Now I need your mind on the game; I need you frosty and ready; because Brian is still out there and we must find him and ring the life out of him to save Silky. I am not going home until he is dead; how about you?" Jazon said.

"No, I won't go back until he is dead and tore apart before my eyes." Ajay whispered.

"Good. We are going to drink this whole bottle; and then we are going to go kill Brian...agreed?" Jazon asked.

"Agreed."

The twin hunters as the Irish people called them; did indeed drink the entire bottle. Strangely, neither was drunk when they opened the door to find their crew armed and ready to roll. Jazon handed them the unopened bottle and told them to pop it and pass it around once they were back on the train.

"Where we going JW?" Terry asked.

Jazon smiled and pulled a cell phone out of his pocket and handed it to Ajay. Ajay smiled and pushed send. The phone connected to Brian instantly.

"So are they dead; they should be dead; I sent enough of those worthless mercs after them. I mean how many can Jazon kill really. It is a good thing his wolves are weaklings or they might have actually gotten me at the albino's house. Why are you not saying anything?" Brian asked.

SHANE

Both werewolves started to speak; but they stopped at a hard look from Jazon. Ajay smiled and spoke into the cell.

"It is because he has not head Brian. You see Mark failed to tell me what I wanted to know' so now he is dead and rent apart. It is important that you know Jazon can and will kill anything or anyone you send against him; and please keep thinking my wolf boys are weak; it will make it much easier for them to kill you pathetic minions." Ajay whispered.

"Who...who is this?" Brian said in a shaky voice.

"I want you to know I am going to stick my gaff in your mouth and blow the top of your head off; and then I am going to cut off your fingers and toes one at a time. I am going to cut off your manhood as well. You can save yourself from all of that Bro, by telling me how to stop the poison my girl has in her body. I will release you from the blood hunt we are on and you can live your messed up life anyway that you see fit." Ajay said.

"I am not afraid of you; and I heard that Jazon was slain; so you are alone." Brian answered.

(laughter)

"Dream on jackass; if my shadow does not get you I sure as hell will. I am immortal Brian; but your not. You might elude me for a short time; however with Collin's network; I will have you in my hands in a short time; a very short time. We are coming Brian; you should either help save the girl; or you should start running right now." Jazon said.

Brian did not answer; there was a strangely growl and then the sound of a cell phone being smashed. Jazon smiled. The wolves did not.

"Why did you tell him about Collin's help?" Terry said furiously.

Jazon laughed, and so did Jc. Everyone else seemed confused. Jazon looked at Ajay and spoke.

"We have a limited time to get that bastard right?" Jazon asked.

"Yah, so?" Ajay replied.

"Simple really brother; we can search the world for Brian or we can drive him to the nearest super power; since Collin is our friend who does that leave?" Jazon smiled as he finished.

"Man, you are on sweat smart mo-fo bro. I can't believe you could set that fool up so easily." Ajay chuckled.

"I want to put my boot in his back at least as much as you do, and If we can take him down hard; then the rest of these blood sucker bastards will think twice before entering my yard for any reason." Jazon said.

The boys plus three strays jumped on a train that just happened to have Erik on it. The dining car is where the crew spent the entire train back to London.

SHANE

They ate and slept there. The other patrons did not seem to mind at all. Terry and Kelli stayed by themselves in the private car. I know what your thinking; and you are only partly right. Werewolves go from childhood to maturity the first time they change. Terry has been considered an adult for two years; moreover, he is one of the best pure combat or melee fighters the packs have ever produced. Kelli made her first full change while the boys packed their small amount of gear. Terry took Kelli out to run as a werewolf. Kelli was glorious to look at; her fur was a soft red-gold and her eyes were werewolf black with aqua rings around the black. Elegant is the only word for how she looked as a wolf-girl. Kelli walked over and put her head against Jc's chest and then Jazon's chest and looked him in the eyes. Later, she would swear absolute loyalty to Jazon; right after her bond with Terry. Jc said this was appropriate; because Jazon was the leader of the entire magical community that they belonged to. Jc told Jazon and Terry that Wolf was going to be pissed that Kelli swore loyalty to a non-wolf; Jc scoffed; because he swore loyalty to Jazon and Ajay as well. Terry said if Wolf didn't like; he was welcome to try to take Kelli from him. The energy that suddenly was in the air would have lit a city. Terry had changed from the reckless mouthy kid into a formidable man; and then Terry was still learning from Jc and Jazon about combat techniques and power usage. From Ajay he had learned courage and sacrifice, honor and valor. Terry respected Jazon's shadow as much as he did the vampire who was his friend and leader. Kelli was an unknown quantity; her natural beauty was now enhanced by pure animal magnetism. The humans that Kelli met on the train were helpless to resist her

SHANE

charms. Kelli was a sweaty and it was not her nature to toy with people but she enjoyed being the bell of the ball. After thirty minutes on the train Kelli went to Jazon and asked him if Terry and her could go cuddle up in the private car. Jazon smiled and squeezed her hand and told her not to break Terry. Kelli giggled innocently and left.

The train ride to London was uneventful. Jc commented that it was likely due to the fact that the last merc army died; went unpaid if they actually survived; that is not a good advertisement for hiring new cronies. Erik had a few bottles of fine wine that he cracked open and served free of charge. The railway company had made a huge settlement from the insurance of the chopper incident. Therefore they had gave Erik a big promotion and made him the head of all the dining services for the company. Erik was only on the train to meet and serve Jazon and his crew; he considered it to be a honor. Payton and Connor were treated as adults because of the life they had led and the fact that Payton gunned down a werewolf that was trying to kill Erik on the first train ride. Erik also witnessed the deadly knife tossing skills of the young man; so when he was told the older boy was his brother and possessed the same skills, Erik was overjoyed to serve them as the heroes they were. Connor was strangely quiet as first; then he asked his brother a question.

"Hey Payton; who is paying for all this stuff?" Connor asked.

SHANE

"Jazon takes care of all the bills. He is the head of a huge organization. The scum we are hunting was the Prince of Portland; but no more. Jazon and Ajay took them down with some help from the wolf pack." Payton said pointing at Jc.

"Do you trust them?" Connor asked.

Payton turned his hard young eyes on his brother for a moment and then he looked at Ajay when he spoke.

"You see that guy; he is just like us Connor; a human. Ajay is like us in another way; he will not stop or cower in the face of danger; he won't hesitate to jump into a hopeless battle; if you are in danger; then he won't stop unless he is dead from trying to save you. No injury, no pain, and no one can make that man turn from what he believes is right. I have decided that he will be the measure of the man I want to be; because is all man and full of honor and courage. I told you all of that; so that you will understand these men. Ajay is the weakest among there ranks in brute strength; but only that nothing else. Every member of there crew will fight and kill for every other member; even if it cost them their lives. Yes, I trust them; I trust them with more than my life. I trust them to guard your life as well." Payton explained.

"How do you know P?" Connor asked.

(chuckle)

"I was picked up in the streets of London by Terry. We were immediately attacked, they grabbed me as the

SHANE

bullets flew and save my life. On the train; a chopper opened up on the car we were in with a chain gun; Jazon jumped in front of me when I was sure I was dead; he took a back full of bullets to save me from harm. In the castle Amus nearly killed me; Jazon grabbed me out of the way before the bullet could kill me. Connor I can go on; these men are heroes and they inspire me to be like them. You have to choose to trust them; but more importantly, you have to earn their trust and loyalty." Payton explained.

Jc and Jazon heard the entire exchange; and Ajay was lip reading the boys so he knew as well what the topic was; none of them commented. Connor would either choose to be one of them or he would have to stay on the outside for the rest of his life.

Erik cried like a big baby when the crew said goodbye to him. It seemed to him that he would never see them again. Erik was shocked that Jazon had survived a contest with Collin. Jazon never told the story; that way Collin's power would not be challenge. Ajay told Collin this before they left; and to Collin's surprise Jazon did not mention it. He just shook the Master vampires hand and began to walk away. Collin stopped him.

"Jazon I would like to know your full name." Collin asked.

"It is Jazon Rev Wild."

The look on Collin's face was golden; he looked like he won the lottery and got a kick in the family jewels at

the same time. He never spoke he just burst to speed
and was gone into the house. Since not a soul knew
why he did that; everyone assumed he expected them
to just leave; or he was heart sick that Kelli was
leaving. Kelli can't be parted from Terry once they are
bonded. A bond like there is rare and very powerful.
They will always know where their lover is and if they
are well or hurt or dead. Kelli needed Terry like she
needed air; it was not a choice; but a necessity to
continue living. Later, when the train stopped in London
Kelli walked out in a new dress with her dark red hair in
a ponytail with a yellow ribbon that matched her dress.
Kelli had a firm loving grip on Terry's hand. Terry said a
fond farewell to Erik who was gushing over Kelli. Well
who would not she was splendid to see.

Within a forty minute interval the crew went from the
train to the airport where Alister's plane was standing
by. The pilot asked where they wanted to be taken.
Nobody knew the answer. Kelli showed her immediate
worth by calling Collin and asking where Kahn lived.
Collin did not want to say; because her feared for Kelli's
life and that Kahn would see her and assume that Collin
was making war on Kahn. Kelli snapped his heels
together and told him to tell Kahn that they were
coming then; in that way Collin was not to be blamed.
Collin reluctantly told Kelli where to go.

"Collin said that we need to go to a town in Mongolia
called Chow." Kelli said.

The boys all laughed because they thought she was
yanking their chain. Kelli did not laugh and Terry could

feel her emotions in his own body through their link and he turned to the pilot.

"Can you find an airport or strip to land this bird on near that location?" Terry asked.

"Oh hell yes, I have been there many times. The Kahn has a fab airport of his own there. I will call ahead and request a landing solution." The pilot said.

The pilot did not tell them that Alister knew everywhere they went and that Alister was having them spied on. Secretly Alister was not sure if he should support or try to destroy Jazon's group. After Alister was told that Jazon stood down Collin; Alister decide that for now the wise course would be to appear to back Jazon in everyway.

The flight from London to Chow was long; but shorter than you might think in a super fast private jet. The crew slept the entire time; even Ajay. There was a fight coming and they all knew it. The plane landed just as the sun went down behind the Himalayas. The airport was just how the pilot said it was; it was posh and spanking new to look at. When the plane stopped Connor and Payton were already on their feet; with weapons in hand. Ajay looked at them oddly; but he knew better than to disregard a fellow slayer's instincts. Ajay pulled his coat on and dropped the safety on his 12 gauge autoloader with special shells for baby boys. Jc was standing by the door. Jazon was asleep. Terry put Kelli beside him.

"Protect him with your life; he is one of a kind Kelli. If he wakes up mad and wants to fight, stay behind him; that is the only safe place to be. Boys let's go out and meet the army they sent for us." Terry said.

The wolves stood by the hatch; each had a brother by their hip. Ajay was in the back ready to go. The pilot dropped the hatch and Jc exploded out the hatch and shifted in mid air. When he touched the ground he was 10 ft tall and 500lbs. Terry landed right beside him even bigger than Jc and he was snarling a clear warning to back off. The brother dropped into flank position s right off the each outside of the wolves. Ajay walked down the stairs and cannon in plain sight. Right in front of him was Ming.

"Greeting Ming; I did not think to meet you again so soon' if ever again. Sadly we are looking for the coward Brian Finney still. We know he ran to you and your Kahn for protection." Ajay said in a calm friendly tone.

Ming ignored him completely. He was studying the wolves and the two children beside them. Ming had never in his long life seen any werewolves this big and powerful. The kids had faces of pure granite and they held their weapons in an expert way for killing. Ming looked at Ajay with a mix of disbelief and disgust.

"You have risked much coming here with out permission. I let you have your life in London; why do you toss it away now?" Ming said.

(Growled laughter and snickers from Ajay and Payton)

SHANE

"You seem to be mixed up Asian food; it was you who were face down and defeated at Ajay's feet not the other way around. If Jazon had not spoken for you at that time; you would not be standing here lying your ass off now." Jc said.

Ming realized that Jc was not a normal werewolf and he did not have the upper hand with these people; they could not be bullied or pushed. They were all fighters and they had the battle scars to prove they were always the victor in those passed trial. However, Ming had a hundred warriors with him and all of them were seasoned vampires. The three humans would die and then he would capture the wolves for his uncle the Kahn; yes that was a good plan.

"Attack." Ming ordered.

In less time than it takes for a hummingbird's wings to flap, Ajay shot Ming center mass with his cannon (shotgun). Ming was on the ground wreathing in pain. Terry completely hulked out; he grew another two feet of height and two hundred pounds of muscle. Terry tore into the Asian vampires like a giant lawn mower. Jc grabbed the boys by the backs of the belts and tossed them back beside Ajay.

"Support the shadow; don't let a single tooth or claw touch him." Jc said sternly.

Five vampires jumped on Jc. He swept his clawed hand across them and two died instantly the other three were missing limbs. A new set of vampire dove at Jc with Chinese broad swords; they were surprised when they all had new silver blades protruding from their tracheas. Jc looked over his shoulder and winked at the boys. Terry had taken several arrows in his face and chest; they did nothing but piss him off. The vampire were laying on the ground at his feet in pieces, Terry was no longer going forward; instead he stood his ground daring the vamps to come to him and they did come and come and come.

A hail of arrows went over Terry's head and he snarled out some words. Instantly Ajay grabbed the boys pulled them to his wide chest and spun around so his back was to the arrows as they hit. To the surprise of the vampires and Connor the arrows just bounced. Ajay smiled as he let the boys go.

"Mithril shirt and pants; when the arrows are shit just step behind me next time and you will be fine." Ajay said as he turned to fight again.

"I don't understand." Connor said.

"Think bullet proof vest only way better." Ajay said.

Instantly another volley of arrows came at Ajay, the boy ducked behind him and the arrows bounced off again. Ajay pulled up the Mithril hood that matched the shirt and covered his face when the arrows came. A few vampires took a wide arc around the plane and tried to enter the plane behind the fighting warriors. Just as they stepped on the stairs a golden nightmare came ripping out of the plane and knocked the three vampires senseless. Kelli grabbed the farthest one away by the arm and flung him against the plane rocking it.

SHANE

"WHAT!" came a scream from within the plane.

A well aimed arrow hit Connor in his left thigh; and the sturdy young man grimaced and nearly went down as he shifted his weight off of the injured leg. Ajay saw the arrow sticking right through the boys leg; and he reached down grabbed the arrow head and yanked it the rest of the way through. Connor screamed in pain. Ajay ripped his coat off and draped it over the boys.

"My coat can stop anything short of bullets and hard sword thrusts, so stay under the coat and the arrows will not get you. When we get home I will ask Tad to make you both some Mithril armor so this does not happen again." Ajay said.

Like lightning Jazon came out of the plane. Only one person saw him moving; and that person was not able to fight a man who could move this fast and not with a sword in his hand. Jazon hit the opposing force with his still sheathed sword; and it looked like a tornado hit them. Vampires flew everywhere; as if by magic. Jazon came to a stop with a bare chest and bare feet. A single arrow shot out of the enemy group and it came straight at Jazon's heart. At the very last moment; Jazon moved left and grabbed the arrow out of the air. Jazon's eyes were so fire red that the blue eyes vampire actually started and stepped back.

"Hey shadow; I am bleeding pretty bad; I think the arrow nicked an artery." Connor said in a shaky voice.

"It is okay bro; I got this." Jazon said.

SHANE

Ajay went back to see how bad the bleeding was. Connor was kneeling in a pool of blood. Payton was holding pressure on the wound but it was too bad to be stopped that way.

"Jazon better come here. Wolves protect our back for a minute." Ajay ordered.

All three werewolves placed themselves in a direct line in front of Ajay. Jazon came over and looked at all the blood pouring out; he reached down and placed his finger in the blood and then tasted it. He smiled and spoke directly to Connor.

"No hint of poison at all little brother; I can stop that bleeding but; you are going to have to trust me; so how about it?" Jazon said.

Connor was a little pale; however he met Jazon's kind eyes with a solid resolve.

"I trust you; help me." Connor said.

Jazon slid his deadly blade out a few inches and then he cut his wrist. Jazon held the bleeding wrist up to Connor.

"Drink it and you will be healed." Jazon said.

Ajay pulled back his hood and smiled.

"It is true; his blood is special; it can cure injuries." Ajay said.

SHANE

Connor looked at them but he leaned in and drank the blood. He was almost stoned looking suddenly. Connor opened his eyes and there was the telling red ring around his pupils; that Ajay had. Anyone who tasted Jason's blood had the sign in their eyes.

"Gasp."

Ajay fell forward and did not move. In the back of Ajay's neck was a tranquilized dart.

"Down in front!" screamed Payton.

The werewolves all hit the deck; all the way to their bellies. Payton stood up and Connor rolled sideways; together they fill the air with thousands of thin silver blades. It would later be referred to as the Silver rain of death. All of the vampires inside of a hundred yards were riddles with blades. That is when Jazon saw Brian Finney. In one move so fast only perhaps Nix could follow it; Jazon grabbed Ming off the ground and then fired him into Brian's back. Before they even hit the ground; Jazon had Finney back the neck and then bone were making grinding sounds in Jazon's hand. Jazon kicked Ming away from them like a football.

"Hello gutter trash. You have less then thirty seconds to live. What did you do to my brother?" Jazon snarled.

"It is only a sleep drug; he will not die. I wanted to distract you so I could get away." Brian chocked out.

"Fine; how do we wake him up Brian; and while we are talking about it; how do we counter the poison you gave Silky Brian?" Jazon asked calmly.

Brian looked suddenly miserable and nervous; and his whole body teased.

"There is no cure; she is dead; but your shadow will be fine; see he is already stirring." Brian said.

Ajay rolled over and yawned hugely. When he looked around his eyes saw Brian being throttled by Jazon. Ajay jumped up and ran over to Jazon. Ming stood up in front of him.

"Ming, I will fight you all you want later; but right now I need to talk with that fool right there." Ajay said.

A small man in red and silver armor said something in an Asian language; Ming looked at him and moved aside to let Ajay go by. Ajay turned and looked at the speaker and gave him a slight head nod or thanks. Ajay walked up to Jazon whose eyes were an inferno of anguished anger. Jazon broke Brian's arms and then he busted his knees. Jazon placed Brian on his busted knees and stepped back.

"How do I save my baby; what kind of poison is it that you used. Tell me and you live." Ajay said.

Out of the blue Jazon stepped forward and used the edge on his finger nail to cut Ajay's neck by the spot where the dart hit his neck. A little blood came out; Jazon taste it off his finger; and then lick licked his clean finger and rubbed the cut. It closed up by itself.

SHANE

"No poison bro." Jazon said.

Ajay already guessed Jazon was making sure he was okay before it was to late.

"WELL!" Ajay shouted.

"There is no cure to that poison; it was meant for Jazon's woman; not yours." Brian said.

"Do you think that matters coward; we would have come after you if it was Jax that same as we did for Silky. Do you remember what I said I would do to you if you let my girl die?" Ajay said.

"Yes."

Ajay rammed the shotgun in Brian's mouth and blew the top of his head off; and then he pumped two rounds through Brian's chest; obliterating his heart and lungs.

"Payton." Ajay said holding out his hand toward the boy.

Payton threw something into Ajay's hand. Ajay caused the object to make a popping sound; and then he dropped it in the hole in Brian's chest. The entire body was ignited. The object was of-course a WP grenade.

"Let's mount up crew." Ajay said as he walked slowly head down back toward the plane.

Jazon however looked right at Kahn; and then he walked over to him. The two men stood looking at each other with hard eyes and firm jaws. Ming was about to speak; however Kahn made a hand gesture and Ming looked afraid; Ming remained silent. Kahn was waiting obviously for Jazon to speak.

"I appreciate your allowing justice to be done; where Brian was concerned. Thank you. I am sad that your men forced us to harm them; we only wanted Finney for his crimes." Jazon said.

"You beat my men without ever pulling your sword young man; may I see it." Kahn said in a very pleasant voice.

Ming looked sick and afraid again; however he did not move at all. Jazon spun his sword and handed it to Kahn without any hesitation. Kahn pulled the sword and his eyes glowed and he smiled. He swept the sword around in a series of arches and dips and then he re-sheathed the blade.

"I know this sword; it is called Soul Stealer and it has never known defeat." Kahn said in a baiting tone.

"Nor will it ever know defeat in my hand either." Jazon said.

(Laughter)

"You are either very brave or incredibly powerful young man. I think we shall have to watch you and see which it is." Kahn said as he handed the sword back to Jazon.

SHANE

Jazon smiled at him and then made a small bow before he spoke.

"We are not finished; you and I are we?" Jason asked.

SHANE

AFTER EFFECTS

In the days that followed Jazon and Ajay's journey; tales were told of incredible deeds and insane tasks; and impossible battles. The only problem was too many people knew that it was actually all true.

Collin was sitting in his castle going through his family tree; and tracing every line on a hunch that he was sure could change the face of the world as he knew it. Collin had not felt hope like this in centuries. Collin knew that Jazon's crew was in London and they would be going back to America soon; he wanted to go bid them farewell and hopefully to meet again. Collin also was mustering his forces because of the issues that were caused by Brian Finney running to Kahn for protection. Strangely enough the Kahn let Ajay kill Brian without interference. Collin knew Kahn well enough to know he was going to exact some price for what the boys had done. Collin also knew that Jazon would slaughter him if his family was attacked; and Collin decide he was with Jazon no matter what.

Back home in the Couve; the Hotel Magical staff was gearing up for the boys to come home. Jax was so excited that she could barely run the nightclub; and help out with the hotel issues. Pegi on the other hand had a handle on it all; she shouted orders and gave out assignments. Alister was already aware that the boys were returning in one piece. He was insane with curiosity; Jazon and his crew had stood up to Collin and Kahn and were all alive; it was unbelievable. Alister

SHANE

wanted to never cross Jazon; not ever. Megan decide Alister needed to take her as his mate and she was not going to take no for an answer. Not to mention Megan was a personal friend to a actual dragon; who said if she needed him; he would break to world apart to come to her. Megan did not want to grow old; she wanted to be young a scorching hot forever.

The Kahn had never seen anyone who was as strong as Jazon and so young. Kahn decided he must get to know everything about this man; before he destroyed him' or perhaps captured his loyalty and could use him to rid the Kahn of Collin for good. Ming had faced the Americas twice and both times he was tossed aside as a non-threat. Ming was not and easy prey for any man or creature. Kahn was clearly intrigued by the young one. It would be best to just kill him before he gain to much support. Kahn knew it was not a good idea to try to get to Jazon through his family; all that would do it get Kahn killed and his territories taken over. No, guile was the right course to deal with this new super predator.

Terry sat with Kelli in his powerful arms as she slept. Terry knew that he was going to have to put Wolf on his back if he tried to tame or force Kelli into his pack. Kelli was his; and with Jc as his wing man; not a single alpha and beta could stand against him. Terry sat waiting for Ajay to say it was time to depart for home; hoping against all odds that Wolf and Enoch don't challenge him. Wolf is like a father to him and Enoch was the wolf who taught him how to fight and survive. Neither of them knew what he could do; or for that matter how much stronger Jc was than either of them.

Jc was in deep thought about Terry. The younger man was an alpha male; hell so was Jc. If push came to shove Jc could likely defeat even Terry; however Jc would never let it come to that; he does not want to be the king. He is more like the Merlin to someone's Arthur.

Ajay was just plain heart broken. He was trying to stay busy; he did not have to think about going home and watching his lover slowly drift away. Jazon had not spoke a word to him since Mongolia; Ajay was not surprised; after all it was his fault they went on this wild goose chase.

Jazon's heart was troubled. Silky was still dying; and Ajay hated him for it. Jazon had been away from his lover for so long she likely did not want him anymore. Now worse, the adventure they just went on; has likely brought the wrath of a powerful vampire lord on the entire families heads. Jazon felt like such a failure. He would find a way to keep his family safe even if it cost him his life.

SHANE

CHARACTERS OF THE NIGHT:
TERMINOLOGY

Jazon Rev Wild: human/vampire, day light vampire light brown hair, brown red or blue eyes, or white with red pupils when he becomes a super vamp 5'7, 148, super fast and strong, immune to sunshine, garlic, holy water, crosses, and is for God he unlikely servant, hero.

Ajay Rey: human, black fella, 5'10, 200lbs, pro ball player, Jazon's best friend , vampire hunter

Jax Kroft: human, female, Jazon's lover, bartender, 5'5 110lbs, short red-black hair green eyes, perfect body

Father Mick Sully: pastor, 55, 5'9 245, grey hair, human, Jazon and Ajay's support coordinator

Reverend John Bishop Jr.: Sully's boss in the church 56yrs old, son of a minister, became a minister early in life very dedicated to the lord. Our GOD

Mark O'Day: Irish vampire, red hair, 5'4 140, dirt bag, killer coward, bit Jazon and turned him

Collin O'Day: Vampire master,1200 year old Jazon's great, great grand uncle, on his mother's side, Mark's great Grandfather

Wolf Peters: Human/werewolf Jazon's ally and friend, golden brown hair 5'10 175lbs, 8' 400lbs in wolf form

Tad Orielly: gnome, 4ft, 150lbs, 600yrs old good guy, Armorer, elite magic user, and battle hardened warrior

Bryan Finney: Vampire, Jazon's enemy, 6', 185, blond, pale blue eyes, charming murderer, Prince of Portland

SHANE

Silky: wood nymph, 5ft, 85 lbs, Ajay's on the side monster gf, green eyes, tan skin, brown hair, good side

Pegi; female human,(205yrs old) semi hillbilly, tough ol lady, funny, no bs type, not afraid of anything, helps Ajay support Jazon, ½ elf ½ human hedge-witch. Her magic is as powerful as anyone on the planet.

Bizerc (Biz): Human hybrid, brown hair, green eyes (sometimes Red) quiet, mysterious, Wolf's friend and Jazon's ally, the boy is the home to a powerful fire demon (a redeemed soul) the boy is immortal because the demon is

PAT Marks: Human, A local Butcher, Christian, helper of Jazon and father sully

Enoch: giant werewolf. Black man, black eyes, bald, deep voice, scarred up.

Gilly⊗ old vampire, insane, blood eyes, shaved head. 6', 200lbs, uses many different blades to kill, hates guns. Used to be a sailor in the 1700's (killed in the first book by Jazon in combat)

TERRY: WEREWOLF, 15 years old, brown hair 6'3 220 as a human, 400lbs in wolf form. Smart mouth, trouble maker, good fighter. Super wolf when pushed

Kelli: Irish werewolf: 15yrs, she is a small; with shoulder length dark brown hair and light blue-green eyes. She is Terry's soul mate and lover. She is also Collin's adopted daughter.

Block: Troll 12ft 1000lbs, green brown skin, smells like apple pie for an unknown reason. strong as a bulldozer and immortal, cant be killed by anything know. He is a good guy, very polite and protective.

Jc: Werewolf shape shifter, 3 forms, pure wolf, Werewolf and skate punk. Shady and fun, age unknown

SHANE

DEMI⊗ the human girl Brian Finney held hostage over Jc, so that the werewolf would do his bidding, she died of starvation, she refused to be Jc's down fall

Alister the White; 560yr old vampire, blue eyes , white hair, handsome, kind of a human lover. He is the one vampire friend Jazon has. Very powerful and respected.

ORSON SWELLS: fat vampire lord over 1/3 of California, old, smart, cowardly.

Lars Mense: thin mouse faces vampire lord over 1/3 of California, old, mean, tricky

Robert Owens: vampire, 40-ish, funny, tough as nails, lords over 1/3 of California and the speaker for all three clans, if it comes to it, he is on Jazon's side.

Amus Savage: human wine and Vineyard master for Collin O'Day 45 yrs.

Patrick Savage: the first human servant and friend of Collin O'Day

Elaura Savage: Patrick's baby sister and best friend. She came to love Collin like a second father even when she was old. Collin extended her life by slipping her drops of his blood in her wine. Elaura died at 197yrs old

Payton: Irish thief, family killed by Mark O'Day. 12yrs old, red-ish hair, blue-green eyes. Assassin class fighter, uses deadly pure silver palm knives

Connor: Irish, rouge, 15yrs old, lost family to Mark O'day, thinks Payton dead. He is out for blood. Becomes Ajay's and Jazon's partner in Ireland. He does not trust them though

Kahn: the ruler of Asia, vampire, quiet but not silent. 5'5, 175lbs, blue eyes. Ming's uncle.

Ming: Chinese, 5'9 190, vampire blue eyes, very surly

SHANE

Kalesar: (Kal) male elf, warrior priest, 6'6 200lbs, long blond hair pointy ears, and soft aqua eyes, good guy. Also call the Indestructible Elf, strongest magic user alive, Tad and Blocks bestfriend

Winky: Werewolf girl, 5ft, 105lbs, brown hair, brown eyes, shy, loyal, Wolf daughter

Nixander (Nix) Gelf (1/2 elf ½ gnome) he is the grandson of Tad. He is a locksmith and junior wizard, 4ft 90lbs can move to fast to see, genius problem solver.

Megan: human, brown hair , brown eyes, 5'11, 115lbs, happy, sexy, smart as a whip and madly in love with Alister.

Sunrise: Yellow dragon, bigger than a bull elephant. He is able to speak the human language; he befriended Megan who named him. Age unknown

Erik: human: Scottish, burly, head cook on the train, made friends with Terry and the boys, very good man.

Burst to speed: (term) verb, it means that a person is moving so fast the human eye cannot follow it, from a stand-still to a blur instantly.

Immortal: (Term) noun: it means a person or being that lives forever and cannot die.

Eternal: (Term) noun: it mean a that a being lives for an extended period of time without aging. Commonly mistaken for being immortal. Vampires and werewolves are Eternals.

The Wild Time: it is the period right after a werewolf is turned, they are extremely emotional and feel the call of the beast that is within them, if they give in to it as a young wolf they will loose their humanity completely and be a mindless killer.

ABOUT THE AUTHOR:

Shane was born Dec 21st, in Portland Oregon, to his mother Toffy Lee Wilson and Oscar Joel Wilson. He has an older sister Cookie Caroline Sinclair and a younger brother Curtis Casey Wilson.

Shane currently lives in Vancouver Washington with his Wife of over twenty years, Arlene; and he son Joston and his daughter Jessica Lee.

Shane races Quads and has won 12 over all championships. Joston has won two and Jessica has one title to her credit as well.

Shane has studied Martial arts for nearly thirty years and has a 5th degree black belt in KAJUKENBO.

Shane loves to entertain people with his stories; so her beautiful wife bought him a laptop and told him to put them all to paper. It is Shane's goal to write 100+ books and publish them all. At his current rate; he will reach his goal in under ten years time.

Shane offers this bit of advice:

"IF YOU THINK YOU CAN; THEN YOU ARE RIGHT. IF YOU THINK YOU CAN'T THEN YOU ARE ALSO RIGHT. THEREFORE, NEVER LET ANYTHING BEAT YOU!"

MY PERSON MANTRA IS:

I CAN'T BE BEAT; BECAUSE I WONT BE BEAT.

I MAY NOT ALWAYS WIN, BUT I NEVER LOOSE.

GOD BLESS YOU AND I LOVE YOU.

BTW: STAY TUNED FOR BOOK THREE

SHADOW GUARD

SHANE